Madame Blini

"I see a woman," Madame Blini said. "A tall dark woman. She is of noble blood. She is a princess. No, not a princess. A queen. An ancient queen. A fearless queen who fought bravely for herself and her people."

"Oh!" Mitzi gasped. . . . "I want to be brave and fearless just like her instead of a mouse like me."

There was a long pause before Madame Blini spoke again. "That should not be hard."

"Why not?" asked Mitzi.

Madame Blini flung off the shawl that was covering her head and looked at Mitzi with eyes that burned like black fire in the candlelight. "Because," she said, staring at Mitzi, "because she is who you once were."

Look for these and other APPLE PAPERBACKS in your local bookstore!

Tarantulas on the Brain
by Marilyn Singer

The Friendship Pact
by Susan Beth Pfeffer

Sixth Grade Can Really Kill You
by Barthe DeClements

Veronica Ganz
by Marilyn Sachs

Cassie Bowen Takes Witch Lessons
by Anna Grossnickle Hines

Oh Honestly, Angela!
by Nancy K. Robinson

Dede Takes Charge!
by Johanna Hurwitz

MITZI MEYER, FEARLESS WARRIOR QUEEN

Marilyn Singer

AN
APPLE
PAPERBACK

SCHOLASTIC INC.
New York Toronto London Auckland Sydney

To the fearless Sandi Singer

Acknowledgements

Many thanks to Steve Aronson, Brenda Bowen, Andrew Ottiger, and Karl Ottiger.

Scholastic Books are available at special discounts for quantity purchases for use as premiums, promotional items, retail sales through specialty market outlets, etc. For details contact: Special Sales Manager, Scholastic Inc., 730 Broadway, New York, NY 10003.

ISBN 0-590-40464-4

12 11 10 9 8 7 6 5 4 3 2 1   7 8 9/8 0 1 2/9

First Scholastic printing, September 1987

1

Mitzi Meyer was hiding in the girls' room. She'd been hiding there for over an hour. It wasn't a very interesting girls' room. There was hardly any graffiti on the walls, and Mitzi hadn't brought a single thing to read.

They'll be back soon, she thought. They'll come get me. Then I won't be bored anymore.

But she didn't know which was worse: being bored or having to face the kids in her class — especially Diane Foster, Bobbie Bolen, and Tracey Dudeen — the Monkey Trio. The Monkey Trio was Mitzi's name for them ever since she'd seen a picture over her dad's desk of three monkeys labeled "Hear-No-Evil, See-No-Evil, and Speak-No-Evil." When Mitzi looked at the monkeys, she thought of Diane, Bobbie, and Tracey, except they were "Hear-Plenty-of-Evil, See-Plenty-of-Evil, and Speak-Plenty-of-Evil." The Monkey Trio would have plenty to say about Mitzi today.

Mitzi sighed and thought back to last week when

Mrs. Livetti, her teacher, had told the class about the trip they were going to take. "On Friday, April 18, we're going to visit Bentner Tower. Bentner Tower is a monument to Josiah Bentner. Does anyone know who he was?"

Mitzi raised her hand. She liked to answer questions in class. But Mrs. Livetti called on Margie Fridley.

"He was a Quaker," Margie said. "And he had a big stable of horses — Morgans."

The class tittered. Everyone knew Margie was crazy about horses.

"Very good, Margie," Mrs. Livetti said. "And what did he do?"

Mitzi raised her hand again, but this time the teacher called on Ricky Horton, whose hand wasn't up.

"He . . . uh . . . bought some land and made it into a nature reserve," Ricky answered.

"*Pre*serve," Mrs. Livetti corrected.

Ricky was the most popular boy in class, and nobody laughed at him when he made a mistake. But Mitzi saw the tips of his ears turn red.

"And that's right, Ricky," Mrs. Livetti continued. "The tower is forty feet high. From the top of it we can see four states. Can you name them, Mitzi?"

Mitzi opened her mouth to answer, but before she could get out a word, Diane Foster said, "Mitzi won't see any states from the top of Bentner Tower. Mitzi will be hiding in the girls' room."

The class giggled.

"That's right, Mrs. Livetti," put in Bobbie Bolen. "Mitzi'll never make it to the top of Bentner Tower. Mitzi's scared of heights."

The class giggled again.

Then, to complete the trio, Tracey Dudeen, in her lazy, sophisticated voice, said, "Mitzi Meyer's not just scared of heights. Mitzi Meyer's scared of everything — including her own shadow."

This time the class really roared — except for Mitzi herself and her best friend, Janet Jellinco. Mrs. Livetti made them all be quiet, but it was too late for Mitzi. She felt terrible.

I'll show them this time, she thought. I'll climb right to the top of old Bentner Tower with everybody else.

She told herself that over and over until the big day came. Just before she left her house, she looked longingly at the book she was halfway through. Maybe I should bring it along just in case. . . . She shook her head. No. No, I won't need it. I'm fearless. I'm the most fearless girl in the world, and I'm going to make it to the top of that tower.

She felt fearless, too, on the whole long bus ride there.

"Are you really going to climb Bentner Tower this time?" Janet asked her.

3

"Yes. I am," Mitzi answered fearlessly and firmly.

The bus pulled up into the parking lot in Bentner Park. Fearlessly, Mitzi hopped off the bus. Fearlessly, she marched up the path to the tower with the rest of her class. Fearlessly, she climbed the first thirty-nine steps (there were three hundred and two in all). Then she took one look out the little narrow window and saw the ground fifteen feet below. Her face began to flush, her palms began to sweat, and the rest of her went cold all over. She ran back down the stairs and into the girls' room as fast as she could.

And that's where she stayed.

I wish I were in the museum, she thought, flaking a chip of paint off the clean walls. I wish I were with *Her*. Then she heard footsteps. "Here they come," she said aloud and sighed.

"Mitzi, you in there?" It was Janet.

Mitzi heaved another sigh, this time one of relief. "Of course I am. Where else would I be?" Mitzi said glumly as Janet came into the room.

"Mrs. Livetti was worried. She didn't know you were missing until we got all the way to the top of the tower. But Tracey said she'd seen you go into the girls' room."

Tracey — who else, Mitzi said to herself. "Did you get to see all four states?" she asked.

"Yes. But they all looked the same. Lots of trees and farms. We saw Lake Wannawanna too. It was

4

pretty. But you didn't really miss much. . . ."

That was Janet, always trying to make Mitzi feel better. Like that time the class took a trip to Wowee Amusement Park and Mitzi was too scared to go on the roller coaster. She wanted to ride the Kiddy Caterpillar instead. It had always been her favorite. But she knew she'd look really dumb doing that. So she stayed on the ground eating her cotton candy while Janet and the other kids went on the Typhoon. Mitzi watched the roller coaster slowly rise to the top of the first hill; then, *whoosh*, down it flew. She could hear everyone yelling, and she had to close her eyes because just watching the roller coaster gave her goose bumps. Finally the ride was finished and Janet came over.

"Whew, that was gr—" Janet began. Mitzi knew she was going to say "great," but she changed it to "gruesome." "Really gruesome. You were smart not to go on it," Janet told her.

But Mitzi knew she'd really loved every minute of the scary ride and that she didn't want Mitzi to feel bad. Janet was a good friend — even if she did have wacky ideas sometimes.

Now Janet was doing the same cheering-up thing. There's probably a great view up there and Janet had a great time, Mitzi thought. And I missed it. As usual. "I really was going to climb the tower this time," Mitzi blurted out miserably. "I thought I was going to be fearless, but I'm still the same

5

old Mitzi Meyer. Mitzi Meyer the mouse."

"Oh, Mitzi. You're not a mouse. You just get scared sometimes. Everybody does."

"You don't."

"Sure I do. I'm scared of lots of things."

"Name three."

"Bees," Janet said promptly.

"Yeah, okay," Mitzi said. She'd seen Janet run away from a bumblebee just last week. "What else?"

"Needles, shots."

"You're not scared of those. You don't like them, but you're not scared of them. I was with you when you got your booster shot, remember. I was the one who ran out of the room," said Mitzi.

"I *am so* scared of them. Just because I didn't say I was doesn't mean I'm not."

"Okay. But what's the third thing?"

"Uh . . ." Janet thought for a long time. "Uh. . . ."

"I knew it!" said Mitzi. "See, you're only scared of one thing. Two, if you count needles, and I don't. But I'm scared of everything." Mitzi stopped talking.

Janet did, too, for a while. Then she said slowly, "Maybe you weren't always scared. Maybe you were once very brave."

"Who, me? Not as far as I know. Dad says I was the scaredest baby he ever saw."

"I don't mean when you were a baby. I don't even mean in this life. I mean in a past life."

Mitzi gave her a funny look. "A what?" she said.

"A past life. A life you lived before this one."

Mitzi shook her head. Janet was at it again. "Are you nuts?"

"No. Haven't you ever heard of reincarnation?"

"You mean the idea that I was once a tree or a dog or something like that."

"Yes — or a person. A *brave* person."

"Hmmm." Mitzi thought about it. Then she said, "Nah, I don't believe it. If I was brave once, how come I'm such a chicken now?"

"There's probably a good reason for that," Janet answered.

"Yeah? What is it?"

Janet thought. Then she said, "I don't know. But I'm sure it's a good one."

"Ha," said Mitzi.

"Is there a good view in here, Mitzi?" Tracey Dudeen interrupted their conversation.

Mitzi looked up to see Tracey Dudeen. With her, as usual, were Diane Foster and Bobbie Bolen. Mitzi hadn't heard them come in.

"There must be," Diane Foster responded. "She spent a long enough time looking at it."

"We knew you wouldn't make it to the top of Bentner Tower," Bobbie Bolen added.

Then Diane said, "Mrs. Livetti told us to get

7

you. We're going to have our picnic now in the park. Do you think you can make it down from here?"

"Tell her we're coming," Janet said.

"All right," said Bobbie, "but don't be long."

The Monkey Trio trotted back out.

"I bet I know what they were in their past lives," Mitzi muttered.

"What?" asked Janet.

Mitzi began to scratch herself and make ape faces.

Janet giggled and joined in.

They left the girls' room laughing. And Mitzi felt a little better.

2

How was your field trip?" Mitzi's mother asked over dinner.

"Okay," Mitzi said, not looking up from her mashed potatoes. Her nose was itching. She wrinkled it.

"Where was this trip to?" asked Mitzi's dad.

"Bentner Tower."

"Oh?" Her father's eyebrows rose, but Mitzi didn't notice. She was still focusing on her food. "Did you climb it?"

"My class did," Mitzi said carefully. She rubbed at her nose.

"Did you climb it with them?"

"Jeff . . ." warned Mrs. Meyer.

"Part of the way," Mitzi answered.

"Which part?" asked Mr. Meyer, ignoring his wife.

"To the first landing."

"The first landing! Oh, Mitzi. What are we going to do with you?" her father said, exasperation in

9

his voice. "You've got to get over these fears of yours."

"Jeff!" Mrs. Meyer said more firmly.

Mr. Meyer looked at her. "I'm not saying these things to make Mitzi feel bad, Michelle. But Mitzi will never get any fun out of life if she's afraid of everything."

Mitzi's head dipped even lower toward her plate. She rubbed at her nose again. Her father probably didn't mean to make her feel bad when he talked that way, but he always did.

"Look at Michael. He's not afraid of anything."

Mitzi's nine-year-old brother frowned. He liked his big sister. She almost never hassled him, and she always came to his Little League games to cheer him on. It bugged him when their dad picked on her.

"And Annie's going to be fearless, too." Mr. Meyer gestured at his younger daughter, who, at two years old, wasn't paying any attention to the discussion at all.

"I wouldn't mind Annie being a little less fearless," Mrs. Meyer said. "I turned my back on her for thirty seconds today, and when I turned around I found her climbing up on the window ledge. It's a good thing the window was closed."

Mr. Meyer didn't say anything for a moment. Then he said, "Mitzi, how about if you and I take our own trip to Bentner Tower tomorrow. We'll climb it together. I'll hold your hand the whole way. You'll see. You won't be scared at all."

"I'm busy tomorrow, Dad," Mitzi said.

"Doing what?" He asked.

"I'm going to . . . the museum."

"That's nice, Mitzi," her mother quickly said. "Are you still working on that Greek vase project for school?"

"Uh . . . sort of," said Mitzi. Actually, she'd finished it a week ago, but she didn't want to say that.

"Then we'll go to Bentner Tower on Sunday," her father said.

Mitzi felt her stomach sink.

But her mother rescued her again. "You can't go on Sunday, Jeff," she said. "You're playing golf with Al DeLiso."

Mitzi's father made a face. "How did I let myself get roped into that one? I'm lousy at golf, and Al DeLiso's a big bore."

"A big bore with a lot of money to invest in your company," Mrs. Meyer said.

Mr. Meyer frowned again. Then he said, "I guess we'll have to take that trip another time."

"Not if I can help it," Mitzi muttered.

"What was that?"

"I said okay, Dad," Mitzi said.

She glanced at Michael. He gave her a sympathetic smile. She tried to smile back, and her

11

still itchy nose twitched. Mitzi the Mouse, she thought.

The next day Mitzi didn't feel like having breakfast with anybody — especially her father. Mr. Meyer was an early riser, a "morning person," he called himself. So Mitzi had to get up practically at dawn to avoid him.

She made her own breakfast, ate it quickly, and was gone before her dad got out of the shower. She congratulated herself on her success. Then she realized she had another challenge. The museum didn't open until ten o'clock. It was now seven-thirty. What could she do for two and a half hours?

I can't go to Janet's. She sleeps late on Saturdays. I don't have any other friends to visit because I don't have any other friends. And I didn't take my book again. If I had my book, I could go to the park and read. But I don't — and it's too early to go to the library to get another one.

"Yoohoo, Mitzi!" a fluty voice called from across the street.

Mitzi looked up. It was her neighbor, Mrs. Pleasant. The name fit her very well. She was a good-natured woman with silver hair and round, pink cheeks.

Mitzi crossed over to her. "Hello, Mrs. Pleasant," she said.

"You're up early today, Mitzi, aren't you?"

"Yes. A little. Are you?"

"Me? No, I've been getting up with the birds for the past seventy-five years. Couldn't oversleep if I tried."

Mitzi smiled.

"So, where are you off to at this hour?"

"Uh . . . I'm . . . uh . . . going to the museum."

"The museum? Doesn't that open at ten o'clock, or have they changed the hours?"

"No, they haven't changed them. I'm . . . uh . . . just . . . uh . . . getting an early start," Mitzi said feebly.

"Hmmm." Mrs. Pleasant paused a minute. Then she said, "Do you have a little time to spare before you go to the museum?"

"Uh . . . I guess so. Why?"

"Because I was just about to work on my vegetable garden, and I sure could use some help."

"Oh. Okay," Mitzi agreed quickly. She'd never gardened much, but it always looked like it might be fun.

"Isn't it too early in the season to plant vegetables?" she asked. "Mom doesn't start our vegetable garden until next month."

"It's too early for some things, but not for others. We'll plant the others."

Mitzi laughed. Then she followed Mrs. Pleasant to the back of her house.

Mrs. Pleasant had a plot of land already staked off. There was fresh topsoil on it, but the soil had to be raked in. Mitzi did that while Mrs. Pleasant went to get the seeds. Next she made neat furrows with a hoe.

"Here you are," Mrs. Pleasant said. "Lettuce, two kinds. Collards. Spinach. Cabbage. And kale. The greens don't mind a little cold weather." She handed three packets of seeds to Mitzi and showed her where and how to plant them.

Mitzi poured a small amount of leaf lettuce seed into one hand. Then she worked her way up one row, carefully spacing the seeds as evenly as she could. When she finished the packet, she felt pleased with herself. Gardening *is* fun, she thought. I wonder why I never did it before. She opened another seed packet. She was just about to put a kale seed in the ground when she saw a very fat and very slimy worm wiggling there.

"Arrgh!" She jumped.

"Mitzi! What's wrong?" Mrs. Pleasant raced over to her. For a woman in her seventies, she could move pretty fast.

"That . . . that . . ." Mitzi stammered.

Mrs. Pleasant looked down, puzzled. "Are you scared of that earthworm? Don't be. He's a gardener's friend."

"He's not my friend!" Mitzi yelled.

"Here." Mrs. Pleasant picked up the worm.

14

"Eww!" Mitzi squealed.

Mrs. Pleasant deposited the worm in another part of the garden. "It's all right. The worm's gone. Now you can do the kale."

Mitzi nodded and started to plant the seeds. But gardening wasn't fun any longer. Every time she put a seed in the ground, she was afraid another slimy worm would rear its head (or was it its tail?) at her. She was glad when the kale packet was empty and she only had the spinach left to go. She finished that as quickly as she could and told Mrs. Pleasant she had to leave.

"Oh, that's too bad," Mrs. Pleasant said. "I was going to offer you some homemade muffins."

Mitzi was very fond of homemade muffins, but she thought it would sound funny if she told Mrs. Pleasant maybe she could stay after all. Mrs. Pleasant would know it was just for the muffins. So she left.

There was still another hour before the museum opened. Mitzi was wondering if there was some way she could sneak back into her house and get her book, when Ricky Horton came jogging up to her. Everybody in her class liked Ricky. Mitzi did, too. He was cute and friendly and a very good athlete. He and Mitzi had never talked much, but sometimes Mitzi noticed him smiling at her — especially when she answered a question in class.

"Hi, Mitzi," he said now. "Where are you going?"

"The museum," she answered.

"The museum? This early?"

"Well, uh, not yet. I was . . . uh . . . just wondering what to do till it opens."

"You want to come with me to pick up my bike? I ran it into a ditch the day before yesterday. Twisted some spokes. Mr. Dixon's fixing it."

"Is he open already?"

"Yes. He opens at eight-thirty. Come on. I'd like some company."

All his friends must be asleep or away, Mitzi thought. Otherwise why would he want me to come along? But because he really was friendly, Mitzi said, "Oh, okay."

They walked toward Mr. Dixon's bike repair shop.

"That was a good trip yesterday, wasn't it? Great view."

He didn't notice that I didn't get to see it, Mitzi thought. "Mmm," she mumbled, hoping he'd take it to mean yes.

"But I wish next time instead of climbing the tower we could climb the cliffs."

"The cliffs!" Mitzi yelped. She hadn't meant to, but the cliffs were high — really high. Five hundred feet in some places. "That's too dangerous," she said in a calmer voice.

"Not with the right training and equipment," Ricky said. "My dad's taken me rock climbing a

16

couple of times. How about you? You ever done any rock climbing?"

Mitzi stared at him for a moment. Is he making fun of me, she thought. Me, Mitzi the Mouse? Didn't he hear the Monkey Trio making fun of me in front of the whole class? But aloud she said, "No. But I've done lots of rock sitting." She didn't know why she made that joke. It was a pretty dumb one. Ricky, however, seemed to think it was funny. He laughed until Mitzi had to join in.

They reached Mr. Dixon's. Ricky's bike wasn't ready yet. "Soon, soon," Mr. Dixon told him. So Ricky and Mitzi hung out on the curb.

"Why are you going to the museum anyway?" Ricky asked conversationally.

Mitzi couldn't very well give him the same excuse she'd given her parents about the Greek vase project since he'd turned his in the same time she had. "Uh . . . well . . . I . . . uh . . . I've been . . . uh . . . thinking of becoming an artist," Mitzi said. Well, she thought, it isn't really a lie. I have been thinking about becoming an artist. And a chef. And a computer programmer. I just haven't made up my mind yet. "So I'm . . . uh . . . studying some paintings there." That wasn't exactly a lie either. Except it was only one painting, and Mitzi didn't think studying is the right word for what she was doing.

"Oh, that's neat. You sure know a lot about art."

"I do?"

"Yeah. You answered all those questions about those vases a few weeks ago."

Mitzi was surprised he'd noticed. "I . . . uh . . . like to answer questions . . . Uh, what about you? What do you want to be?"

"Me? I'm thinking of studying marine biology. I'll have to learn to scuba dive first, though."

Mitzi smiled at him. But inside, she thought, scuba diving, rock climbing — Ricky's just like Janet. He's not afraid of anything either. Even old Mrs. Pleasant isn't scared of things. She picked up that disgusting worm without a second thought. I really am hopeless.

"Here's your bike, Ricky," Mr. Dixon said, wheeling it out. "As good as new. Almost."

"Thanks, Mr. Dixon," Ricky said. "What do I owe you?" He paid the bill and got onto the bike. "Want a ride to the museum?" he asked Mitzi.

Mitzi would have loved a ride. The museum was a long walk away. But she was scared to get up on the handlebars. "Uh . . . no thanks, Ricky. I . . . uh . . . walking's good exercise."

"Yeah, it is. Well, see you around." He pedaled off.

Mitzi watched him ride away and twitched her nose mouse-style. "Squeak, squeak," she said and, with a sigh, scurried off to the museum.

3

At precisely ten o'clock, two uniformed guards opened the doors to the Chillington Museum of Art and let Mitzi inside. There were only a few other people there that early, so Mitzi practically had the whole place to herself.

The museum was not a large one — and Mitzi knew exactly where in it she wanted to go. But she held off, just the way she opened the prettiest wrapped birthday present last or saved her French fries until after she ate her squash to make the pleasure last longer.

One gallery in the museum was devoted to a new exhibit every six weeks. There was a display of Early American quilts there now. Even though Mitzi didn't care about quilts, she went to look at them first. To her surprise, they turned out to be more interesting than she thought they'd be, and very colorful too — all those little pieces of fabric carefully stitched together to form stars or birds or houses. Mitzi especially liked one called a "crazy

19

quilt," which described it well — patches and patches of velvet, satin, gingham, and calico, all put together in a bright, crazy pattern. Looking at it, Mitzi remembered her third grade teacher, Mrs. Wilson, telling them about quilting bees. A bunch of women and girls would get together hour after hour to chat and piece together a quilt. Mitzi could imagine them doing it. She could almost imagine herself doing it, too. Part of her liked the idea a lot. It was so safe and soothing. No towers to climb, no roller coaster rides, not a worm in sight. Something even Mitzi the Mouse wouldn't be afraid of doing, she thought.

But there was another part of Mitzi Meyer. A part that didn't want to sit around doing something safe and soothing. A part that Mitzi wanted very much to let everyone see if only she knew how.

Mitzi took one last look at the quilt and, without waiting any longer, hurried out of the gallery. She walked quickly through some other galleries, where marble sculptures stood on pedestals and paintings full of splashy colors and weird shapes hung on the walls, until she came to one particular room. This room had only pictures of people. Mitzi knew each of the portraits pretty well. She nodded at the scholar in his black robes, smiled at the fat woman with the baby on her knee, said hello politely to the boy in fancy green knickers, hurried

20

away from the sour-faced man in his stiff-collared suit. Finally she came to a painting in the far corner of the room. It wasn't a particularly large painting or an especially bright one. In fact it was rather dim and stormy. It wasn't painted by a famous artist, either. But Mitzi didn't care about any of that.

What she did care about was the figure in the painting. It was a tall, strong woman with wild, dark hair that streamed out behind her. She was riding in a chariot pulled by four horses. Riding straight into battle. Printed beneath the picture, was her name: *Boadicea — Queen of the Britons*.

Mitzi had first discovered the painting on a class trip to the museum — one of the few class trips she'd thoroughly enjoyed. The class was studying ancient Greece, so Mrs. Livetti and Mr. Morales, the art teacher, took them there to look at the collection of Greek vases. Each vase had a different scene from Greek life or mythology on it. All the students were to pick their favorite vase and write about what it showed. Mitzi asked — and answered — a lot of questions about the vases, the myths, and the history of Greece. She chose a vase that showed a group of women dancing because she herself liked to dance. Janet picked one in which people were drinking wine, and everybody teased her about it, but she didn't mind.

After they looked at the vases, the class got to

tour the rest of the museum. Mitzi had been there before, but she hadn't really looked closely at many of the paintings. When they got to the portrait gallery, Mitzi's eyes wandered around the room until they landed on Boadicea. Zap! It was as if the queen's own hand had reached out from the painting and pulled her over. "Wow!" she said under her breath.

She stood, wide-eyed, staring at the fierce queen. She was so captured by her that she nearly forgot she wasn't alone in the gallery.

"Is that a relative of yours, Mitzi?" Diane Foster asked.

"Her mother, maybe?" said Bobbie Bolen.

"There is a slight family resemblance," Tracey Dudeen added.

Mitzi didn't say anything. She didn't want the Monkey Trio to know that she was thinking there actually was a resemblance.

"Let's see what everyone's staring at here," Mr. Morales said, saving her from having to say anything at all. "Why, it's Boadicea, the Warrior Queen. She nearly succeeded in freeing Britain from Roman rule."

Mitzi listened closely to what Mr. Morales had to say about Boadicea's exploits, but the Monkey Trio kept staring at her, so soon she sauntered away, trying to appear no longer interested in the painting. The truth was she was even more interested in it. She went back to the museum the next day to look at it, and then a few days after that.

And here she was again. Today was her fifth visit. And she wasn't tired of Boadicea at all. She stared long and hard at the picture. She could see the queen's horses' hooves pounding, her chariot wheels turning. On the spokes were knives, nasty, sharp knives to cut and slash the enemy to ribbons. Clouds of dust blew up from under the wheels that turned faster and faster. Boadicea's whip cracked.

Suddenly, Mitzi felt the wind roaring all around her. Her hair blew wildly about her head. Instead of Boadicea, it was she who was in the chariot, the whip in one hand, the reins in the other.

"We will beat back the barbarians!" she shouted. "We will free the land! We will never be Roman slaves!"

"Ha ha."

"Ha ha?" Mitzi said. She blinked. Who was laughing? It wasn't Mitzi. And it wasn't Boadicea. She blinked again. She was no longer in the chariot. She was sitting in front of a small painting on the cold, hard museum floor. And standing next to her were two little kids pointing at her and giggling.

"Jody, Jackie, stop that. It's not nice," their mother tried to shush them.

Mitzi, blushing, scrambled to her feet and hurried out of the room, past a tiny woman in a red dress and a security guard in a too-tight uniform. She scurried down the corridor, through the front door and down the museum steps.

When she reached the street, she took a big breath. Daydreaming again, she thought. But it seemed so real this time. Like it was me in that chariot instead of Boadicea. Me who was brave and strong. Mitzi felt a chill of pleasure run up her back.

And with as much dignity as she could muster, she straightened her spine, held her head high, and marched down the street toward Janet's house.

4

"You went to the museum again," Janet greeted Mitzi.

"How'd you know that?" Mitzi asked, settling herself down next to her friend on the bed.

"I called your house. Your dad told me. He sounded like he was sort of bugged with you."

Mitzi sighed. "Last night he asked me about the field trip. I had to tell him I couldn't climb the tower. He wanted to take me there today so we could climb it together to help me stop being scared of heights." Mitzi made a face. "I told him I was going to the museum instead."

"Gee, Mitzi, maybe that's not such a bad idea — going to the Tower with him. You could climb it real slowly. You wouldn't have to keep up with the class."

"No. I'd just have to keep up with my dad. You know what he's like. He thinks he's patient, but he's not. Not at all. Remember when he was supposed to coach the softball team and the pitcher was really bad? Dad couldn't stand it, so he ended up pitching himself. Or how about the time he was supposed to teach me how to ride a bike? I fell a couple of times, but he was the one who quit. My mom won't even go skating with him anymore. She wobbles, so she likes to go slow. But Dad doesn't and he practically drags her around the rink. He'd drag me right up Bentner Tower, too, if I went with him."

Janet looked at her sympathetically. "I guess it wasn't such a good idea after all." Then she asked, "Did you have a good time at the museum?"

Mitzi hesitated a moment, then nodded.

"You went to look at that painting again." Janet was the only person Mitzi told about her interest in Boadicea. She even went to look at the painting a couple of times with Mitzi. Janet thought the portrait was nice, but she liked the one of the boy in the fancy green knickers better. However, she thought Mitzi was entitled to her own taste.

"Yes," Mitzi answered slowly. "And this weird thing happened. I felt like it was me in the painting this time, instead of Boadicea."

"Wow!" said Janet. "Maybe you had an out-of-the-body experience. That's where your spirit leaves your body for a while and goes somewhere else."

"It was more like an out-of-my-head experience," said Mitzi. "I was talking out loud to myself

26

and stuff. Some little kids saw me and laughed. It was embarrassing."

"You shouldn't be embarrassed if you've got special powers."

Mitzi gave her a funny look. "Janet, have I told you that you sound a little strange these days."

"I'm not strange. Lots of people believe in this stuff. I'm reading a book all about it. It's called *Is There Life After Life After Life?*"

Mitzi snickered.

"Go ahead and laugh," Janet said coolly. "I've got to go sign up for junior lifesaving at the Y. Do you want to come with me?"

"The Y? I was just near there," Mitzi groaned.

"You don't have to if you don't want to." Janet was still being cool.

"I'll come." Mitzi sighed. "Just as long as I don't have to sign up for swimming lessons again." She remembered her first and only lesson. She climbed down the wrong ladder into the deep end of the pool. The teacher had to fish her out, choking and sputtering. She ran for the showers, stayed there until the class was finished and then fled the Y, never to return.

"Oh, it's too bad you don't want to take swimming lessons," Janet teased. "I could use you for the body in my lifesaving class."

"Very funny," Mitzi said. "Let's go."

* * *

27

It didn't take Janet long to sign up for her class. Mitzi was glad about that. She felt uncomfortable in the place. The chlorine smell that seeped into the registration office from the pool next door brought back unpleasant memories of her underwater experience.

"Let's go to McDonald's," she said. "I haven't had any lunch and I'm starved — "

"Hey, Mitzi! Two times in one day," Ricky Horton interrupted her.

Janet gave her a surprised look.

"Oh hi, Ricky," Mitzi said, feeling pleased and flattered by his friendliness.

"Did you get to study the paintings you wanted to?"

"Uh, yes."

"That's good. You'll never guess what. Remember how I was talking about wanting to learn scuba diving? Well, I just found out they're starting a scuba class for kids right here at the Y."

"Oh, that's good for you."

"Yeah. The only thing is they need at least eight people to sign up for it. I'm the first one on the list. You want to take it too?"

Janet coughed into her hand.

Mitzi gave her a look. She knew Janet was trying not to laugh. Janet never made fun of Mitzi in front of other people, but she had to think it was pretty funny of Ricky to be asking her if she wanted to scuba dive, for Pete's sake.

"I don't think so, Ricky. I'm, uh, pretty busy," said Mitzi.

Janet coughed again.

Ricky turned to her. "How about you?"

Mitzi clapped her friend on the back — a little harder than usual.

"Ouch," said Janet, then, "Scuba diving, hmmm. When is the class?"

"Fridays at four o'clock. It starts two weeks from next Friday."

"Hmmm. It does sound like fun. I'll think about it," said Janet.

Mitzi frowned. Janet *would* want to learn scuba diving. Especially with Ricky Horton in the class. Who wouldn't want to be in a class with blond, blue-eyed Ricky Horton? Stop it, Mitzi, she chided herself. Don't get mad at Janet just because she's not a mouse like you.

"Great!" Ricky said. "You sure you don't want to, too, Mitzi? I bet you'd like it. And we've got to fill up that class."

Mitzi looked at his eager face and felt bad. She hated disappointing people, especially when it was because she was too scared to do something. Maybe I would like scuba diving, she thought. An image flashed through her mind of herself in a wet suit, flippers, and face mask with a heavy oxygen tank strapped to her back. She was lowering herself off the side of a small boat into the ocean. She drifted down, down, down into the black depths.

"No!" she gasped and shuddered.

"Gee, okay. I guess you're really too busy," said Ricky.

Mitzi blinked and focused on him. He had a sort of hurt, confused look on his face. Mitzi realized he thought she'd shouted at him. She wanted to apologize, but before she could, he said to Janet, "Well, I hope you decide to take the class. If you know anybody else who might want to, tell them to sign up right away," and he left quickly.

Mitzi and Janet left, too, and Mitzi didn't say anything until they were almost at McDonald's.

"Oh, Janet. I'm such a nerd," she said. "Now Ricky thinks I yelled at him, and he's been so nice to me today, too." She explained to Janet how she and Ricky had met earlier and gone to the bike shop together.

"Don't worry. You can tell him what really happened next time you see him," Janet soothed.

"I guess." But Mitzi was thinking she didn't really want to tell him what happened, that she was scared of scuba diving, scared of everything. Ricky was the only person she knew who didn't seem to think she was a mouse, although she couldn't for the life of her understand why. She didn't want to tell him the truth. You're dumb, Mitzi, she said to herself. He's going to find out anyway one way or another. Everyone else has. The thought made her very sad.

"Oh, Janet. Why *am* I so scared of everything?" she said.

Janet didn't answer. She just patted her friend on the back.

The two girls went into the restaurant, ordered their cheeseburgers, fries, and Cokes and took their trays to an empty table near the window. There was piece of paper, a flier of some kind, at Mitzi's place. She pushed it aside and set down her tray. Janet sat down across from her. Mitzi sipped her Coke slowly. She didn't feel much like talking. She was thinking of Boadicea again and the way she'd "gone inside" the painting.

All of a sudden, Janet let out a yell. "Kismet!" she announced. She was holding the flier in her hand.

Mitzi jumped. "Janet, you just made my soda go up my nose."

Janet didn't apologize. "Kismet," she said again, waving the piece of paper.

"Kiss who?"

"Kismet. It means fate, something that happens because it's supposed to. Like this."

"Like what?"

"This. The solution to all your problems."

"Huh?" said Mitzi. "What are you talking about?"

"Look. Read it," said Janet.

Mitzi took the sheet of paper and read it out loud: " 'Be the person you want to be by knowing the person you once were.' Huh?"

"Keep reading," Janet said excitedly.

" 'You may not know it, but you have been here before. In another time. In another place. In another body. Perhaps you were rich. Or famous. Or brave. You can be all that again — and more. Let Madame Blini uncover your past lives to help you with your present one. Come see her today. Call 555-6336 for an appointment. Madame Blini — 'The Future is in the Past.' ' "

Mitzi finished reading and looked up. "Janet, what problem is this supposed to fix?"

"Mitzi, this is what I was trying to tell you about yesterday. You were once a different person. Look at this part. 'Perhaps you were rich. Or famous. Or *brave*.' See? Madame Blini can uncover your past life and tell you about how fearless you were once. You may not believe me, but you've got to believe her."

"Why? Why do I have to believe her?"

"Because she's a psychic. A genuine psychic."

"A *psycho*?"

"No, a *psychic*. Someone with special powers to see the past and the future."

32

"I thought you said *I* have special powers," said Mitzi.

"Well, you do. You just haven't trained yourself to use them like Madame Blini has. . . . Oh, Mitzi, I just know she can help you. I can sense it in my third eye."

"Your what?"

"My third eye. My center of psychic sensitivity. It's right here." Janet tapped her forehead.

"Oh, let me see," Mitzi said mysteriously, crossing her eyes. "Why, yes. You're right. There it is. I can see it with my special powers that I've just trained myself to use."

"Oh, Mitzi," Janet said. "Don't be such a skeptic. I'm going to call Madame Blini for an appointment myself. Do you want to make one too? We could go together."

Janet was so enthusiastic Mitzi didn't have the heart to say no. "Uh, I'll think about it," she said.

"Okay. But let me know soon. Madame Blini may not be here too long. She may feel the call to move on to another place."

Tomorrow, with luck, thought Mitzi, but instead of saying that, she went back to finishing her Coke.

5

The next morning, Mitzi slept late. The house was quiet when she opened her eyes. The light filtering through the lowered shade in her bedroom was pale gray. I hope it's cloudy, she thought, yawning and stretching. She rolled slowly out of bed, went over to the window, raised the shade, and looked out at a washed-out sky. Good, she said, smiling to herself.

As far back as she could remember, Mitzi liked cloudy days. They were cozy. No one expected her to do anything outdoors — scary or not scary — because it might rain any minute. So she could indulge herself in her favorite indoor pursuits such as reading, cooking, dancing, and daydreaming. Then, later on, she could go to the movies (which, cleverly enough, was what she and Janet had planned for that afternoon). The best cloudy days were when Mitzi's parents were out doing something and she (and Janet or Michael) had the place

34

to herself. That didn't happen often.

But today Mitzi was in luck. After she did her morning exercise routine (ten toe touches, twenty-five push-ups, and running in place for five minutes), she got dressed and went down to the kitchen. Michael was there, reading a baseball magazine. They gave each other the elbow knock greeting they'd seen a couple of the New York Mets give each other on TV.

"Hey, Mike," she said.

"Hey, Spike," he answered. It was a private joke between them, one not even Janet or Lenny, Michael's best friend, knew about.

"Where's everybody?" Mitzi asked.

"Dad's playing golf."

"Oh yeah, that's right. I hope it doesn't rain on him."

"Mom and Annie are visiting Cousin Pam." Cousin Pam lived in the same town just a few streets away. "Mom said they'll be back in an hour or so, which means at least two hours or maybe three."

Mitzi laughed. When Mom and her cousin got to talking, no one could stop them. "Well then, I guess I'll make myself some breakfast."

"What are you going to make?" Michael asked with great interest.

"Gee, I don't know. Oatmeal, maybe," Mitzi said nonchalantly, avoiding her brother's eyes.

"Yuck," he said.

"Or maybe. . . ." She paused. "Pancakes." This time she stole a glance at him.

He was practically drooling. "Uh, Mitzi, do you think you could make me a couple, too?" he asked.

"Why? Didn't you have your breakfast already?"

"Yeah. But you know I always have room for your pancakes."

"You always have room for anything," Mitzi said with a grin. But she was really pleased that her brother liked her pancakes. They were one of her specialties — and she had quite a few. But pancakes were her favorite. She liked to invent new varieties — banana/pecan, apple/sunflower seed, strawberry/rhubarb. As she got out the ingredients, she started thinking about what kind she'd make today. But her mind drifted to the *idea* of pancakes instead. When did people start eating pancakes? Who invented them? Are they an ancient dish? Did Boadicea eat them? She got the familiar little chill of pleasure when she thought of the dark queen. She closed her eyes for a moment and could almost see herself in the chariot again. . . .

"Mitzi, isn't the flour supposed to go in the bowl instead of on the floor?" Michael's voice interrupted her.

She jumped and looked down. She was slowly

pouring a powdery white stream from the sack in her hand on to her mother's clean linoleum. "Whoops," she said, quickly righting the sack. She was glad it was just Michael who'd caught her daydreaming this time and not her parents or some strangers. "I better sweep this up before I start making the pancakes."

"I'll do it," Michael hurriedly said. "So you can cook."

"Thanks, Mikey," Mitzi said, with another grin. He was really dying for those pancakes.

She got out the rest of the regular ingredients and opened the refrigerator. What can I make this time, she thought. Tuna fish pancakes? Yuck. Beet pancakes? Nope. Avocado? Hmmm. Pears? Now there's an idea. Pears with walnuts. And some interesting spice like — ginger. Yes, that's it. Humming, Mitzi began to chop, pour, and mix.

"Do you mind if I watch you this time?" Michael asked when he'd finished sweeping.

Mitzi shook her head.

He stood near her and watched. He knew she didn't like to talk while she cooked, so he kept quiet.

When the pancakes were ready, Mitzi dished up two stacks and carried them over to the table.

"Excellent," Michael said, taking a big mouthful.

Mitzi smiled.

They ate in friendly silence.

"More?" Mitzi asked when Michael had finished his.

"Yes, please," he said. "Hey, maybe you could teach me to cook sometime."

"You really want to learn?"

"You bet."

"You don't think it's too much of a girl thing?"

Michael shook his head. "Mitzi, you have some weird ideas sometimes."

Mitzi chuckled. "That sounds like something I said to Janet yesterday."

"I'll teach you something in return if you want."

"Like what?"

"What do you want to learn?"

"How about how to be brave," Mitzi said in a kidding voice.

Michael didn't say anything for a moment. He knew when Mitzi was really joking — and this was only half a joke. "Dad shouldn't have gotten on your case like that yesterday," he finally said quietly.

Mitzi sighed. She was sorry she'd brought up the topic, but it was too late now. "Yeah. But I can't blame him either. Everybody in this family is brave except me. I don't fit in. Sometimes I wonder if maybe I'm adopted."

"Sure. Or maybe they found you in a basket at the front door," Michael said deadpan. "Or wrapped in tissue paper under the apple tree."

"Michael," Mitzi warned.

"Hey, no. I got it. They found you in a grocery store. That explains why you're such a great cook."

"Michael!" Mitzi said, but she started to giggle. Her brother joined in.

Then Mitzi said, "All right, so I wasn't adopted. But I'm still the biggest coward in this family."

"Oh, I don't know," Michael said. "Remember how we used to play 'rescue'?"

" 'Rescue'?" Mitzi gave him a puzzled look. "No. What's that?"

"It was a game you made up. You'd pretend you were a soldier or a magician or a queen and I'd be in danger — like tied to a stake about to be shot or burned or eaten by a dragon — and you'd rescue me."

"Huh? I don't remember that. You're making it up."

"I am not. One day, I wanted to switch and rescue you, but you wouldn't let me."

"Michael, I would've remembered if. . . ." Mitzi broke off. A dim memory was surfacing. She was wearing a long cape and brandishing a plastic sword. Michael was tied to a bedpost with a couple of shoelaces. "I am a warrior queen," she was saying, as she cut through Michael's bonds to free him.

"You were saying . . ." Michael teased when he saw her expression.

"I made that up," she said with wonder.

"Uh huh. You were real brave then."

Mitzi didn't speak for a moment, then she said, "But that's just it — I *made it up*. I wasn't really brave. Only in my head."

Michael shrugged. "What's the difference?" he said.

Mitzi gave him a strange look. "Oh, Michael. Come on, there's a big difference."

Michael shrugged again.

"I gotta go meet Lenny," he said. "You want me to do the dishes first?"

"No, it's okay. I'll do them."

He nodded. "Thanks for the pancakes. They were great." He tucked his magazine under his arm and trotted out of the kitchen.

Mitzi sat at the table another moment. "Rescue," she murmured. "Funny I didn't remember." Then she got up and began to do the dishes.

6

Janet was waiting impatiently in front of the Strand Cinema. Mitzi could tell she was impatient from a whole block away because she was tapping the ground with her foot and patting her leg with her hand. Janet wasn't usually impatient, but Mitzi thought this time she had a good reason to be because Mitzi was fifteen minutes late.

Mitzi walked faster, pumping her legs so hard the muscles hurt. She felt like she'd never reach her friend. But at last she did. "Oh, Janet. I'm so sorry. I was . . . uh . . . thinking and I lost track of the time. I hope the movie hasn't — "

"Mitzi, boy, am I glad you're here," Janet cut her off. "I'm sorry, but I just couldn't wait."

Mitzi wrinkled her brow. "Huh? You mean you saw the movie already?" she said, confused and wondering if she'd misjudged the time even worse than she'd suspected.

"The movie? Oh no, I mean Madame Blini. I know I said we could go together, but you didn't call and I was dying to see her. So this morning I called for an appointment and she said to come right over."

"You went today?"

"Yes. Don't be angry with me, Mitzi. I just had to go."

"On Sunday morning?" Mitzi said, thinking Madame Blini kept strange business hours.

Janet misunderstood. "Oh, you are upset." She frowned.

"No. No, I'm not. What was she like?"

Janet's face lit up. "Oh, she was wonderful! She has great powers. I could feel them *emanating* from her when I walked into the room."

"Emma-what?"

Janet didn't explain the word. Instead she went on, "Before I even sat down she said, 'Waterchild.' Isn't that something?"

"It's something, all right," Mitzi said dryly.

"See, she knew I swim a lot, and I hadn't even told her. Then she had me sit at a table across from her. 'What is it you wish to know, my dear?' she asked. I told her I wanted to know my past so I could understand my future. She nodded. She took my hands and gazed into my eyes. And then you know what she said — "

"Movie starts in two minutes. You girls going in?" the woman in the ticket booth called out.

"Yes. Yes, we are," Mitzi said. She hurried over

to the window with Janet in tow and plunked a couple of dollars down on the counter.

Janet did the same, talking the whole time. "She said, 'You were here many times before. You are an old soul.' Isn't that beautiful?"

Mitzi didn't think "beautiful" was the right word, but she didn't say anything.

The two girls walked into the theatre and handed their tickets to the ticket taker.

"You want some popcorn?" Mitzi asked at the refreshment stand.

"Unh-uh." Janet shook her head.

Mitzi bought herself a small box.

Janet went on talking, "Then she said. . . ."

"Uh-oh. Music. The movie's starting. Come on." Mitzi hurried through the double doors into the darkened theatre with Janet following her. Sure enough, the credits were just rolling on the screen.

"Then she said, 'You are here again to learn and to teach.' Isn't that great!" Janet said, too loudly.

"*Shh*," someone hissed at her.

"Sorry," Janet apologized.

"It's packed in here," whispered Mitzi. "Can you see two seats together?"

Janet looked around. "There," she said. "Near the front on the side."

"Oh, that's so close," Mitzi grumbled.

"I don't see anything else," Janet whispered back.

They made their way down the aisle to the second row. To get to the seats they had to step over several pairs of legs. Mitzi did a balancing act with her popcorn. She made it to her seat without a spill and gave a sigh of relief.

"So she knew because of my past lives I was a teacher and I'm going to be one again," Janet said as soon as she was seated.

"Janet, the movie's on," Mitzi said.

"*Shh*," shushed someone behind them.

"Sorry," Janet apologized again. "We'll be quiet." She lowered her voice to a whisper. "Mitzi, she was really terrific. I think she could help you a lot. And she only charges five dollars."

Mitzi didn't answer. She focused on the screen and raised a handful of popcorn to her mouth. But the person at her other side jostled her arm and she spilled the popcorn down the front of her shirt. She turned her head to give the person a dirty look and saw, by the light of the screen, that it was Ricky Horton.

"Ricky!" she said in surprise. "What are you doing here?"

Dummy, she thought. What do you think he's doing here?

"Hi, Mitzi," he replied. "I'm watching the movie. Did I bump your arm?"

"Uh, yes. You did. But it's okay. I didn't drop much popcorn."

"I'm sorry," Ricky said. He turned back to the film.

The movie was a high adventure. Two girls and a boy had to rescue the kingdom of Anadama from an evil sorcerer. It was just the type of film Mitzi loved. But now she was having a hard time concentrating on it. She still felt embarrassed about the day before when she'd daydreamed about scuba diving and accidentally yelled at Ricky. He must think I'm a creep as well as a mouse, she thought. She wished she could change her seat, but that might be even more embarrassing.

The best thing to do is to apologize, she thought. "Uh, Ricky," she whispered, "about yesterday. I wasn't really yelling at you. . . ."

"Shhh," said Janet. "This is an exciting part."

Mitzi looked at the screen. The boy and girls were trapped in an underground cave. A huge monster with the head of an alligator, the body of an elephant, and the wings of a dragon was coming after them. One of the girls had managed to climb up a stalactite above it.

"Ooh!" Mitzi squealed. "Ugh!"

The girl used another stalactite to stab the monster right between the eyes. The monster fell to the ground, dead. Mitzi, Janet, and everyone else cheered. She forgot about Ricky and all her other problems and got caught up in the rest of the movie.

An hour later, after more thrills and chills, the film ended with Anadama free, the sorcerer vanquished, and the heroes richly rewarded.

"That was great!" Janet said as the house lights came up. "Wasn't it, Mitzi?"

"It sure was."

"Did you like it, Ricky?" Janet asked.

Mitzi blinked. She'd gotten so wrapped up in the movie she'd forgotten he was there.

"Oh, yeah!" he answered. "I really liked that tough girl — the one who killed the monster."

"Me too," said Janet.

Mitzi didn't say anything. She was remembering that she still owed Ricky an apology.

They walked out to the lobby together. Janet excused herself and went to the girls' room. It's now or never, Mitzi thought. She opened her mouth to tell Ricky what really happened, but she never got the words out because Ricky said, "That tough girl reminded me of you, Mitzi."

Mitzi's mouth stayed open. "Of me," she squeaked.

"Yeah."

Mitzi gulped. "You mean I looked like her."

"No, you don't. You sort of *act* like her."

Mitzi stared at Ricky, and, all of a sudden, she began to get suspicious. Something's funny here. Something has to be. I'm not *anything* like that girl, Mitzi thought. Ricky keeps saying these weird things to me. He acts like he doesn't know what I'm really like. Either he's dumb or asleep or crazy — but he doesn't seem like any of those things. Or else he's making fun of me. Mitzi looked at Ricky's open, friendly face and thought it seemed almost impossible he'd be so awful. But she couldn't think of any other explanation. She felt hurt and angry. She wanted to get away from him.

At that moment, Janet returned. Mitzi grabbed her hand. "We have to go," she said, and, pulling her friend past Ricky, she ran out of the theatre as fast as she could.

"Mitzi, what're you doing? Mitzi!" Janet said as Mitzi dragged her up two blocks. "Mitzi, slow down. I'm out of breath."

Finally, another couple of blocks later, Mitzi did.

"What's wrong? Did the movie bug you or something?" Janet asked, falling in step next to her.

"Not the movie," Mitzi mumbled.

"Then are you mad at me for going to Madame Blini's?"

"No. I told you I wasn't mad."

"Well, what is it then?"

Mitzi looked at Janet. "It's . . . Ricky," she said at last.

"Ricky? Ohhh." Janet started to grin an I-get-it grin. "He really is nice, isn't he? And cute and smart. No wonder everybody likes him. I'm surprised he was here alone today. He's always got a lot of friends around him. Maybe he — "

"Nice? Cute? Smart?" Mitzi said, her voice rising and her lower lip wobbling. "Next to Tracey Dudeen, he's the meanest person I've ever met!"

7

"I hate gym. I hate gym. I hate gym. I hate gym,"
Mitzi muttered as she got into her sweatsuit.
Mitzi was in a bad mood. She was still upset at
Ricky. She'd told Janet what he'd done. Janet
couldn't believe he'd be so mean and tried to come
up with another explanation. But Mitzi didn't believe her. Then there was the Monkey Trio, still
teasing her about the trip to Bentner Tower. And
as if all that wasn't bad enough, today in phys ed
they were going to start Mitzi's least favorite thing
in the world — apparatus.

"I hate gym. I hate gym," she chanted again
under her breath.

"No, you don't," said Janet, whose locker was
next to hers. "You don't hate gym when we have
dancing. Or when we play volleyball or softball."

"Well, I hate it now," said Mitzi. "I'm too scared
to vault over the horse or to do swivel-hips on the
trampoline, and I've never been able to climb those
dumb ropes. Every year I try, and every year I
can't budge an inch."

49

"Maybe nobody showed you the right way to climb them. Maybe somebody can."

"Maybe. But it sure won't be Mrs. Vetch," Mitzi grimaced. Mrs. Vetch, tall, thin, and muscular, was a good teacher — *if* you were an athlete. If you weren't, if you were either a klutz or a coward, Mrs. Vetch was not a good teacher at all. She didn't have enough patience. Mitzi thought that Mrs. Vetch was an awful lot like her father.

The second bell rang to start the class. Mitzi gave out one more "I hate gym," and, with a vicious tug at her sweatshirt, she followed Janet out of the locker room.

Mrs. Vetch was standing at one end of the gym next to the trampoline. She blew her whistle shrilly. "Okay, class. Get into your squads."

The class obeyed. There were four squads. Mitzi and Janet were in Squad Four, along with the Monkey Trio, a boy named Jason Pollack, and Ricky Horton.

"Today we start apparatus. For those of you who are new to this school, apparatus consists of the trampoline, the horse" — she pointed to a long, padded thing on legs with two handles sticking up from its middle — "the parallel bars, and the ropes. I will demonstrate to the whole class what you have to do on each piece of equipment. Then each squad will practice on a separate piece. Mr. Rizzo

50

and Miss Walker" — she gestured at the two student teachers — "and I will help you. I'll start with the trampoline. Mr. Rizzo and Miss Walker, will you spot, please."

Mrs. Vetch gracefully mounted the rubbery sheet and began to bounce up and down, lightly at first, then harder. She performed several twists and drops, and finally she sprang into the air and did a forward somersault, landing neatly on her feet.

Some of the students oohed and aahed; some clapped. Mitzi yawned. She'd seen Mrs. Vetch's demonstration several times already. It was nice to watch, but Mitzi got the funny feeling that Mrs. Vetch wasn't just demonstrating — she was showing off.

After the trampoline, Mrs. Vetch showed them how to vault over the horse, first between the handles, next in a half straddle (one leg between the handles, the other leg extended over one of them) and finally the full straddle, with both legs out to the sides. Then came the parallel bars, which she walked across on her hands, and last, the ropes.

"Climbing the ropes is one of the best tests of strength, endurance, and coordination there is. You use your hands and arms to pull yourself up and your legs and feet to hold on and stabilize yourself. If you can climb the ropes, you are a *real athlete*. Instead of my demonstrating, this time I think I'll choose someone else to do it —

Ricky Horton." She smiled approvingly at him.

"Yay, Ricky. Go, Ricky," some of the kids yelled.

Boo, Ricky, Mitzi said silently.

Ricky stepped forward and jumped up on the big knot at the bottom of the rope.

"When I say go, begin," said Mrs. Vetch. "One. Two. Three. Go!"

Smoothly, confidently, Ricky began to climb, reaching, then pulling up with his arms and hands, his legs stretching and bending in rhythm. He reached the top in no time at all.

"Yay!" cheered the class, except Mitzi.

"Excellent," said Mrs. Vetch. "Now, Ricky will show you how to come down. You must never slide down a rope, or you'll burn yourself. You must come down the way you went up. Show everyone, Ricky."

Ricky did, reversing his arm and leg movements. When he touched the ground, everyone cheered again.

"Hey, Ricky! You're a *real athlete*," Diane Foster called out.

"Unlike some other people we know," said Tracey Dudeen, giving Mitzi a sideways glance.

Mitzi felt the anger that had been sitting in her stomach all morning flare up. She wanted to say something nasty back, but Mrs. Vetch tweeted her whistle again and Mitzi's stomach went cold. She knew what the sound meant.

"All right, class. Time for practice," said Mrs. Vetch. "Squad One and Mr. Rizzo — over to the horse. Squad Two and Miss Walker, the trampoline. . . ."

Mitzi held her breath, hoping it would ward off the inevitable.

It didn't. "Squad Three, the parallel bars. You can practice without being observed for a while. And Squad Four, you stay right here with me at the ropes."

Mitzi let out her breath with a sigh. Not only the ropes, but Mrs. Vetch too. I don't have any luck, she thought. The only thing that could save me now is the bell.

"Okay, first two climbers, Pollack and Jellinco," Mrs. Vetch said.

Janet and Jason jumped up on the knot of each rope. "One. Two. Three. Go!" commanded Mrs. Vetch.

Janet climbed the rope nearly as well as Ricky, although not quite as fast. Jason, chubby and short-legged, wasn't so successful. He got about half-way up and couldn't go any further. He hung there, red-faced, while the Monkey Trio giggled.

"All right, come down. Jason, you need to practice more. Next. . . ."

Come on, bell, prayed Mitzi.

"Bolen and Foster."

"Oh, Mrs. Vetch. I can't climb today," Bobbie

said. "I hurt my ankle in class during volleyball last week, remember?"

Mrs. Vetch did remember and she frowned. "Surely it's better by now."

"Oh no, it still hurts a little."

I'll bet it does, Mitzi thought. She could tell Mrs. Vetch was thinking the same thing.

But the teacher excused Bobbie anyway. "All right, then. Foster and Dudeen."

Diane and Tracey took their places on the ropes. ". . . Go!" ordered Mrs. Vetch. And up they went. Diane, agile and wiry, got pretty high up, but Tracey didn't make it even as far as Jason had.

Ha, thought Mitzi. Okay, Ms. Monkey, Ms. Some-of-Us-Are-Athletes-and-Some-of-Us-Aren't. What do you have to say for yourself now?

"Well, gee, I guess I didn't eat my Wheaties this morning," Tracey said.

Everyone laughed. Even Mrs. Vetch cracked a small smile. "Okay. More practice for you, too, Tracey. Come down. Next. . . ."

Oh, where's that bell, Mitzi pleaded silently.

"Well, that leaves just Meyer," stated Mrs. Vetch.

"I'll climb again," said Ricky with a friendly smile.

He's trying to show me up, Mitzi thought. She didn't smile back.

"Fine," said the teacher. "Let's hurry now. Class is almost over."

Mitzi jumped on the knot, trying to ignore Ricky on the one next to hers. She gripped the scratchy rope with her hands and hugged it with her knees.

"Okay. One. Two. Three. Go!"

Ricky went up like a flash. Mitzi reached, pulled hard and went nowhere.

"Go!" Mrs. Vetch ordered again.

Again Mitzi strained with her arms. Her feet came off the knot and flailed in the air.

She could hear the Monkey Trio giggling like crazy. She also heard Janet tell them to shut up, which only made them giggle harder. She refused to look at any of them.

"You're strong, Mitzi," Ricky's voice called down to her. "Use your arm muscles and hold on tight with your legs and feet."

Without wanting to, she glanced up. He was smiling at her encouragingly again. She felt her anger flare up once more.

"The only thing Mitzi knows how to use her legs and feet for is running away," Diane said, and the Trio giggled some more.

I'll show them, she said to herself. I'll show them all. She gave a tremendous heave. Suddenly, she was two feet off the knot and four feet off the ground. "I'll show them. Unh," she grunted and pulled herself up another two feet.

"Hey," she dimly heard Bobbie Bolen say. "She's doing it!"

"Go, Mitzi! Go!" yelled Janet.

"Come on, Mitzi. You can make it to the top," said Ricky.

And Mitzi did. Slowly, with a lot of sweat, she made her way up the rope and touched the ceiling of the gym.

"Yay! Hooray!" Janet and some of the other kids cheered.

Mitzi cheered too. "I did it! I did it!" she yelled. How do you like that, Tracey Dudeen, she thought. How about it, Ricky Horton? What do you think of me now, Mrs. Vetch? Am I a *real athlete* too?

"Okay. Come down," said the gym teacher.

Mitzi dipped her head to look at her and gasped, "Oh no!" She was high up. Very high up. Too high up. Nothing was between her and the ground below but fifty feet of air and one thin, scratchy rope, which she was now desperately clinging to.

"Meyer, come down," Mrs. Vetch repeated.

Mitzi saw that Ricky had already touched the floor and she moaned. How am I supposed to get down? I can't slide or I'll burn my hands and legs. Go down the same way you came up, a voice said in her head. "Right," she said aloud. But when she tried to move, she simply couldn't. Her body was frozen. Whimpering, she swayed back and forth on the rope, getting dizzier and more frightened by the moment. And then the bell rang to end the class.

"Meyer!" Mrs. Vetch hollered. "Quit fooling around and get down here on the double. This class is over."

The class may have been over, but nobody had left. Everyone was clustered around Mrs. Vetch, staring up at Mitzi, swinging on the rope. The Monkey Trio began to titter. So did several other kids.

"I can't come down, Mrs. Vetch," Mitzi called.

"What do you mean you can't come down?"

"I can't move."

"Nonsense. You're not paralyzed."

Oh yes I am — with fear, Mitzi thought. Now she understood just what the expression meant. "I just can't," she repeated. Tears welled up in her eyes.

The class's laughter rose. Janet's loud voice cut through it. "I think she's really . . . uh . . . stuck, Mrs. Vetch."

"Oh, my heavens. What next?" said the gym teacher. "Ricky, go get Mr. Webley, and hurry. The rest of you go change at once and get back to your classroom."

The rest of the class reluctantly went to change, but they managed to peek in the gym afterwards just in time to see Ricky return with the custodian. Together they were toting a huge ladder.

"Jeez, what's this? A circus act?" Mr. Webley said, positioning the ladder near Mitzi. He climbed up. When he got high enough, he reached out with one hand and pulled over the rope. "Okay. Step down now. Easy does it."

Mitzi stepped on to the ladder. It felt solid under her feet, but she was still scared because the ground was just as far away. She eased down the ladder slowly. When she finally got off the last rung, a cheer went up from the doorway.

Mrs. Vetch whirled around. "I said get to class!" The crowd rushed away.

"I need help with this ladder," Mr. Webley told Ricky, as he folded it up. They left together.

Mitzi was alone with Mrs. Vetch. She couldn't look at her.

"Miss Meyer," the gym teacher said. "I don't know what stunt you thought you were pulling, but in all my years as a gym teacher I've never seen anything like it. I'm going to call your parents about this. Be advised."

"Yes, Mrs. Vetch," Mitzi mumbled.

"All right. Now change and get to your class."

Mitzi nodded and stumbled out of the gym. But she didn't bother to change her clothes. Instead, she walked into the hall, straight out the school's front door, and into the street before anyone could stop her.

8

Mitzi didn't care where she went as long as it was far away from everybody she knew. She'd been humiliated before, but not like this. This is the worst thing that ever happened to me, she thought. I'll never be able to show my face in school ever again. A few tears trickled down her cheeks. She brushed them away and kept walking. She walked for a long time.

After a while, she found herself in front of the Chillington Museum. She hadn't thought about going there — at least her head hadn't. But her feet obviously had. She let them take her right to Boadicea.

There was nobody in the room with the dark queen except her fellow portraits. Mitzi didn't even bother to greet them this time. She went right up to the woman in the chariot and blubbered, "Oh, Boadicea!" Then she broke down and cried.

When no more tears came out, she wiped her

eyes. She reached into her sleeve, found an old shredded tissue she'd stuck there, blew her nose as best she could and studied the painting through bleary eyes. "Tell me something," she said. "How come I feel like you inside, but I can't act like you? I mean, I feel brave sometimes, but when I try to be brave, I can't be. Were you brave all the time? Were you a brave little kid?" Mitzi sighed. "Yeah, you probably were. When you lived, you had to be, with all the wars and stuff. We don't have that here, now. But you still have to be a brave kid, or everybody makes fun of you." She began to sniffle again. Suddenly she stopped. She'd heard a noise behind her. She turned her head. But all she saw was a flash of a purple skirt passing by the doorway.

She shrugged and went back to talking to the portrait. "It's no good feeling sorry for myself, is it? You wouldn't feel sorry for yourself. I've got to *do* something. . . . Except I don't know what to do."

She sat quietly a little longer. Then she got up to leave. As she walked toward the door, she almost slipped on a piece of paper lying near it. She bent down, picked it up, and was about to throw it away when she noticed what it said: "Be the person you want to be by knowing the person you once were. . . ." It's that Madame Blini, she thought. That lady Janet went to. Janet's excited words came back to her, "She's really terrific. I just know she could help you."

Mitzi paused in the doorway, still holding the flier. Then she said out loud, "Well, why not? It's worth a try." And with a bob of her head, she headed for the nearest telephone.

Madame Blini didn't answer, and Mitzi tried to convince herself that it was just as well. I must be crazy, thinking this psychic person could help me. Actually, Mitzi was disappointed. Janet had been so certain Madame Blini could help her, and Mitzi felt right now she could use all the help she could get.

She wandered around the museum some more. Then she left and sat for a long time in the little park next to it. I might as well go home, she thought. But before she did, she decided to try phoning Madame Blini once more. One ring. Two rings. Three. Four. Mitzi was just about to hang up when a low, husky voice answered, "Hello, seeker." For a moment she couldn't say anything. The voice on the other end waited patiently. Finally, Mitzi said, "Hello, is this Madame Blini?"

"It is," the husky voice said and paused. Then, "How may I help you?"

"I'd . . . uh . . . I want to find out how to be the person I've always wanted to be."

"Ah, yes." Another pause. "When will you come?"

"To see you? Uh . . . when can I come?"

The longest pause yet. "Friday at one o'clock."

"Friday at one? But that's a long time from now, and besides, I'm supposed to be at school. . . ."

"Then in half an hour."

"Half an hour!"

"Yes. Can you make it?"

"Uh . . . yes . . . yes, I can make it. What's your address?"

Madame Blini told her, finishing with, "It's around the corner from a pawnshop. Knock on the lion three times."

"What?"

"Knock on the lion three times. When you come, you will understand."

"Oh . . . uh . . . okay. See you soo — "

Click. Madame Blini had hung up.

Mitzi looked down at the dead receiver. "In half an hour, I'm going to change my life," she said. Then she added, "I hope."

The town Mitzi lived in wasn't all that large. You could walk from one end of it to another, although it would take you a couple of hours at a fast clip. Mitzi thought she'd been all over the town, but she'd never been to the part where Madame Blini's "office" was. It wasn't one of the nicer areas of town. Not that it was really dangerous, just run-down or "seedy," as Mitzi's dad would call it.

It took Mitzi exactly twenty-two minutes to walk there from the museum. She followed the directions Madame Blini had given her, passing a gas station, an auto repair shop, and a bar before she came to the pawnshop. It was a small shop with a big, grimy window and a crooked sign. Hanging from the sign was a curious sculpture of three golden balls.

Mitzi'd heard of pawnshops — places where you could "hock" some valuable, such as a ring or a radio or a slide trombone. You gave the pawnbroker the item, and he gave you some money. You got a certain amount of time to repay the money and get back your valuable, and if you didn't, the thing went up for sale. Mitzi paused to look in the pawnshop window. It was filled with jewelry, silverware, china figurines, radios, stereos, and musical instruments. Mitzi was admiring a pretty pin that had a thirty-dollar price tag attached to it, when suddenly her hand flew to her mouth. "Money! I don't have any money! I left it back in my gym locker with the rest of my things. How am I going to pay Madame Blini?"

She patted the sides of her pants (even though they didn't have any pockets) and poked up her sleeves (even though she knew she never kept any money there). What am I going to do? I made it all the way here. I can't turn back now. She shook her head.

"Ouch!" she said and rubbed her neck. Around it was a "lucky stone" pendant she'd bought on her family's last vacation to Virginia. Some of her hair had caught in the chain, and it was pinching her. She unclasped it, pulling the hair free. The necklace slid into her hand. The deep blue stone with gold flecks gleamed dully at her. She rubbed her fingers over it. Suddenly she had an idea. "Well!" she said. "You haven't brought me much luck up to now — but maybe this time you will." And without hesitating, she pushed open the pawnshop's dirty glass door and went inside.

A bell tinkled as she crossed the floor to the high counter. But no one appeared. Oh no. What do I do now — "Yikes!" she shrieked. A very thin man with yellow-gray hair, a pinched face and huge glasses popped up from behind the counter. "Yes?" he said, ignoring the fact that he'd nearly scared her to death. "Can I help you?"

Mitzi caught her breath and boldly said, "I want to pawn a necklace."

"A necklace? Do you have it on you?"

"Uh . . . yes," she said. "I do."

"Put it on the counter."

Mitzi had to stand on her tiptoes to reach the

top of it. She opened her sweaty palm and poured the necklace onto it.

The pawnbroker picked it up by the stone. "Just a moment," he said. Carefully, he took off his glasses and put them on the counter. Then he picked up a small eyeglass — the kind jewelers use — and put it to one eye. "Hmmm," he said. "Hmmm. Nice workmanship."

Mitzi felt her heart give a bump. Oh, it's got to be worth at least five dollars, maybe a whole lot more.

The thin man put down the eyeglass and looked at Mitzi. "Three bucks," he said.

"Three dollars!" Mitzi cried. "But you just said the workmanship was nice."

"Yes, it is. It's a nice piece of fakery. A little glass, a little iron pyrite — and presto, lapis lazuli. If it were real, it would be worth fifty, maybe seventy-five dollars. But it's not. So, three bucks. Take it or leave it."

Mitzi was beginning to feel desperate. "Can't you make if five? That's all I need."

The pawnbroker shook his head. "Listen, kid. All I'll get for that myself is five, six bucks. I've got to make some kind of profit. That's what's called business. Besides, I'm not even supposed to deal with kids. So take the three bills and consider yourself lucky."

Mitzi's lip began to wobble. She knew she was about to burst into tears for the second time that day. "Please," she whispered hoarsely. "I walked all the way here just to see Madame Blini. She charges five dollars and I forgot my money."

Suddenly, the pawnbroker's face changed. It looked a little less pinched. "Madame Blini, eh?"

"Yes. Do you know her?"

"Yeah, you might say so." He paused. "Let me look at that necklace once more." He picked it up.

Mitzi didn't know exactly what had happened, but all at once the pawnbroker was friendlier.

"Well," he said. "Maybe I can give you five dollars after all."

"Oh! Oh, thank you!" Mitzi said. She felt like giving him a big hug.

The pawnbroker wrote up a slip. "You have two weeks to redeem this. And you pay me back with interest, of course," he said. Then he opened his cash register, took out a wrinkled five-dollar bill and handed it to Mitzi.

"Thank you!" Mitzi said again. She slipped the pawn ticket and bill into her sneaker and raced out of the shop.

She turned the corner and stopped at the third door on the left. Hanging smack in the center of it was a brass door knocker shaped like a lion's head with a ring in its mouth. "Knock on the lion three times," Mitzi said, remembering Madame

Blini's words. She grasped the ring. "One." She knocked. The sound wasn't very loud. I'd better do it harder, she thought. "Two." There, that was better. She was just about to knock a third time when a wave of panic seized her. What am I doing here at a strange house in a strange part of town instead of being in school? How do I know Madame Blini isn't a maniac or someone who's going to tie me up and make me eat bread and water for days and days? She sounded kind of weird on the phone. Mitzi let go of the ring and was about to run away when she remembered once again that Janet had gone to see Madame Blini just yesterday, and she didn't think the psychic was a nut. She thought Madame Blini could really help Mitzi. And boy, do I need help, Mitzi thought. Taking a deep breath, she grabbed the ring once more and knocked a third time, the hardest of all.

I hope she's not upset that I'm a little late. That business in the pawnshop took a while. Mitzi waited nervously on the doorstep.

Then slowly the door opened all by itself. A husky voice and the strong smell of incense floated down. "Come upstairs."

Mitzi coughed, gulped, and obeyed.

At the top of the stairs, instead of a door, there was a beaded curtain. Mitzi pushed through it, the beads rattling mysteriously as she did. Behind the curtain was a short hallway.

"This way," came the same voice from a room on the right.

Mitzi followed the sound and turned into the room. It was dark. The only light came from three candles on a small table. Mitzi could barely make out the figure sitting behind the table. It seemed to be wearing an awful lot of clothing — not only on its body, but over its head.

"Uh, Madame Blini? I'm . . . uh . . . sorry I'm late. . . ."

"Sit down, Dreamer," the figure interrupted her.

Dreamer? Does she mean daydreamer, which I am, or something else, Mitzi wondered. She stumbled to the chair opposite the figure, bumping her shin on it before she managed to sit down.

The woman across from her didn't say anything else for such a long time that Mitzi began to squirm in her seat. Finally she spoke. "Give me your hands."

Mitzi held out her hands.

From under her layers of clothes, Madame Blini thrust out her own hands and grasped Mitzi's. They were large, warm, and dry.

"Good hands. Brave hands," the great psychic said.

"Huh? Brave? I'm not brave. I'm sc-scared. I'm scared of . . ." Mitzi began.

But Madame Blini cut her off again. "Hands that

have held the reins of a nation have no need to fear."

Mitzi didn't understand what Madame Blini was talking about, but this time she didn't make the mistake of asking her what she meant. She sat quietly, her hands still shaking.

"I see a woman. A tall, dark woman. She is of noble blood. She is a princess. No, not a princess. A queen. An ancient queen. A fearless queen who fought bravely for herself and her people. I see her riding into battle. In her chariot."

"Oh!" Mitzi gasped.

"Her name, the queen's name. It begins with a 'P.' No, that's not right. A . . . 'B'! Yes, that is it."

"Boadicea," Mitzi whispered in wonder. "You see Boadicea."

"This Boadicea. She is special to you. Very special."

"Yes."

"And do you know why?"

"Because . . . because I want to be brave and fearless just like her, instead of a mouse like me."

There was a long pause before Madame Blini spoke again. "That should not be hard."

"Why not?" asked Mitzi.

Madame Blini flung off the shawl that was covering her head and looked at Mitzi with eyes that

69

burned like black fire in the candlelight. "Because," she said, staring at Mitzi, "because she is who you once *were*."

"Oh!" gasped Mitzi once again. "Oh, my!" And she fell right off her chair.

"Remember, and you shall not fear again," Madame Blini finished. "That will be five dollars, please. In cash."

It took Mitzi a moment to understand what she'd said, so Madame Blini had to repeat it. In a daze she took off her sneaker and dug out the five-dollar bill. She put the sneaker back on and got to her feet. Swaying a little, she laid the money on the table in front of Madame Blini.

"Remember," the psychic repeated. And she covered her head with her shawl once again.

Mitzi didn't answer as she stumbled out of the room.

9

Mitzi didn't remember a single thing about her long walk home. It seemed like one moment she was tripping through Madame Blini's beaded curtain, the next she was standing in front of her own house. She didn't know what time it was either — or that school had gotten out two hours ago.

She climbed up the four steps to her porch, pushed open the front door, and went straight to the kitchen. She'd missed lunch and wanted a peanut butter and bacon sandwich more than anything in the world.

Her mother was on the phone with her back to Mitzi. "I don't know where she went, Pam. Nobody seems to know. Jeff and Michael are out looking now. Yes, I called him at work."

Mitzi opened the bread box and took out a loaf of whole wheat bread.

"She was upset. Mortified. She must've just walked out."

Mitzi opened a cabinet and took out a jar of peanut butter.

"Yes, I know, but she's never done anything like this before."

Mitzi pulled open the refrigerator door and got out the bacon. Then she reached for a frying pan, and a bunch of pots crashed to the floor. Mitzi jumped.

So did her mother. "Mitzi!" Mrs. Meyer shouted. "Pam, she's here. Call you back later." She hung up the phone and rushed over to hug her startled daughter. "Oh, Mitzi, Mitzi," Mrs. Meyer babbled. "You nearly scared me to death. Mrs. Livetti called and said you hadn't returned to class after gym. Then Mrs. Vetch called and said something about how you refused to climb down the ropes and that the custodian had to be called in. I couldn't understand what she was going on about until Janet came over just a little while ago and explained. She said you must've been too upset to go back to Mrs. Livetti's class, but she didn't know where you were either. Nobody did — " Abruptly Mrs. Meyer stopped talking and held Mitzi at arm's length from her. "Where were you?" she demanded.

Mitzi didn't say anything for a moment. Finally, she spoke. "I . . . I went to the museum."

"You spent all that time at the museum?"

"Uh . . . I went to the park, too," Mitzi said,

choosing her words carefully so she wouldn't have to lie.

"Oh, Mitzi." Her mother sighed. "I know you felt bad, but you shouldn't have run out of school like that. And then not even to have called — "

"Michelle, we've looked all around the neighborhood and we — Mitzi!" Mr. Meyer said, coming into the kitchen with Michael in tow. "Where have you been?"

"She went to the museum and to the park," Mrs. Meyer answered for her.

"Great! Now we've got a truant for a daughter."

"Jeff, Mitzi was upset — "

"Upset? Upset? Not as upset as she made the two of us. She ran out of school and didn't tell a soul where she'd gone. And all because she was too scared to climb down the ropes in the gym. Mitzi, enough is enough. We've got to do something about those fears of yours. This weekend, no excuses. We're going to Bentner Tower, you and I, and we're going to climb it all the way to the top."

Michael, who hadn't said a thing, looked sympathetically in Mitzi's direction.

But Mitzi didn't return the look. She was staring down at her hands.

The phone rang. Mrs. Meyer picked it up. "Yes. Yes, she's here. She came back. . . ." She looked at Mitzi. "It's Janet."

73

"Tell her Mitzi can't talk to her right now. Mitzi's being sent to her room," her father said.

Mrs. Meyer looked as though she was about to argue, but instead she told Janet that Mitzi was unable to come to the phone. Then she hung up.

Everyone stood there quietly for a moment. Then Mr. Meyer said, "Well, what are you waiting for? Go to your room."

Without a word, Mitzi went.

She sat down on her bed and leaned back against the headboard. She wasn't thinking about her parents (although she was sorry to have upset them) or about Janet or about what had happened in gym. She was thinking about Madame Blini and what she'd said. She thought a long time. And then she didn't feel dazed anymore. She felt thrilled. More thrilled than she'd ever been in her life.

There was a knock on the door. Mitzi drew herself up regally. "Who dares to knock upon my door?" she called out.

"It's me, Michael. Mom thought you might be hungry."

"Enter!"

Michael did, balancing a tray in one hand. He set it down on Mitzi's desk.

"Ah, nourishment," Mitzi announced. Then she grabbed the peanut butter and bacon sandwich off it and took a big bite. "Mom always overcooks the bacon," she said, her mouth sticky with peanut butter. But she devoured the sandwich in two minutes flat anyway, washed it down with a big swig of milk, and started on an apple, pacing the room as she did.

"Dad's really mad this time," Michael said slowly.

"Is he?" Mitzi said. "Yes, I suppose he is."

"I don't think you're going to get out of going to Bentner Tower this time, so, if it's any help, I'll go along too."

"Thank you, dear brother," Mitzi said. "But I shall not need any assistance."

"You mean you've figured out a way not to go?"

Eyes gleaming, Mitzi whirled to face him. "No. I mean I *want* to go. In fact, I cannot *wait* to go."

Michael blinked in confusion. "You cannot?"

"No, I cannot. I'm going to climb up every step of that tall tower, and when I reach the very top, I shall look out over Josiah Bentner's preserve and the states of New York, New Jersey, Connecticut, and Massachusetts, and I shall tell the world, 'Here I am! It is I! I have fought the battle, and I have won!' "

"Mitzi, are you feeling okay?" Michael asked.

"I am well. I am more than well. I am great. I am the greatest, strongest, bravest person in the world!"

"Maybe I ought to leave you alone for a while." Michael picked up the tray and started out of the room.

Just as he reached the door, Mitzi called, "Mike!"

He turned around. Mitzi wound up and tossed the apple core at him. It landed neatly on the plate in the middle of the tray. The dishes rattled, but nothing broke.

"Holy cow!" said Michael.

Mitzi grinned at him. "Hands that have held the reins of a nation have no need to fear," she said as he hurried out of the room. "And I fear nothing. For I am none other than Mitzi Meyer, Fearless Warrior Queen!"

10

There was a lot of buzzing as Mitzi walked into the classroom.

"Just ignore them," Janet whispered, striding alongside her.

"They do not disturb me," Mitzi said calmly, holding her head high.

"They don't?" Janet said with surprise. "I mean, I'm glad they don't."

The two girls took their seats.

"What goes up but doesn't come down?" they both heard Tracey Dudeen say in a loud whisper.

"What?" asked Margie Fridley.

"Mitzi Meyer."

A lot of the kids giggled.

"Oh, shut up," Janet told them.

Mitzi didn't say anything. She just sat very straight in her seat.

The buzzing and laughing continued until Mrs. Livetti came in. She was carrying a small case with holes in it.

"What's in there, Mrs. Livetti?" Jason asked.

"You'll find out soon," Mrs. Livetti answered. She put the case under her desk, got out her book, and took attendance. When she got to Mitzi's name, she looked up, smiled and said, "I'm glad you're back with us, Mitzi."

"What goes up, but doesn't come down?" Diane Foster murmured in a singsong voice.

The class giggled again.

Mrs. Livetti told them to be quiet. "Today we're going to start with science, a brand new unit called 'Animal Locomotion.' " She wrote the words on the blackboard.

There was rustling as the class took out their notebooks and copied the words down.

"Who knows what *locomotion* means? Mitzi?"

"Movement," Mitzi answered with certainty.

"Mitzi knows a lot about movement — in one direction," Tracey said.

"Animals move in a lot of different ways. Tracey, name some."

"Uh, uh . . ." Tracey, taken by surprise, stammered. "Uh . . . walking. And, uh, running."

"Right. What are some others?"

"Flying," Margie Fridley answered.

"Swimming," said Janet.

"Climbing," Ricky said when Mrs. Livetti called on him.

The class looked at Mitzi and giggled. But Mitzi kept her eyes on the teacher.

"Jumping. Hopping," some other kids answered.

"Right," said Mrs. Livetti. "There's one way nobody's mentioned yet. We'll let Bruno demonstrate." She lifted up the case, opened one side of it and took out a three-foot-long snake, which she held stretched out with both hands.

"Oh, ugh!" Diane gasped.

"Yuck," said Bobbie.

"Nas-ty," said Tracey.

Some other kids screamed or gasped or made retching noises. Mitzi didn't make any noise at all.

"This is Bruno. Bruno's a boa constrictor, and he's still only a baby."

"I'd hate to see him when he grows up," said Jason, and everyone laughed.

"Does he bite?" another boy asked.

"No. He has teeth, but he doesn't bite. He doesn't have fangs, which means what?"

"He's not poisonous," a girl named Freda answered. "He kills his prey by squeezing them to death. I know a lot about boas, Mrs. Livetti. My brother has one."

"Ooh. Ugh. Yuck," more kids said.

"That's right, Freda. Now, how does Bruno move?"

"He wiggles," another girl said.

"He crawls," said Janet.

"You're both right. Watch." Mrs. Livetti put the snake on her desk and let him move halfway across it before she picked him up again. "Bruno wiggles and crawls, and he does that by flexing his muscles." The snake looped around Mrs. Livetti's arm.

"Better make sure he doesn't get near your neck, Mrs. Livetti," Jason said.

"Oh, Bruno's too little to strangle me. Boas rarely bother people anyway. But strangling or *constriction* is another kind of movement a snake makes. I'm going to draw a sketch and write some words on the board. Who'd like to hold Bruno while I do?"

"Not me," said Bobbie.

"Not me either," agreed Diane Foster.

"I'll hold him. I know how," Freda said. "I've held my brother's snake lots of times — when my mother wasn't looking."

"Then we'll give someone else a chance to," said Mrs. Livetti.

Suddenly Mitzi spoke up loud and clear, "I shall hold him."

The class turned to her with shocked expressions. Even Janet looked surprised.

Mrs. Livetti smiled. "All right, Mitzi. Come up here."

80

All eyes were on her as she walked with great dignity to the front of the room.

Mrs. Livetti gently pried Bruno off her own arm and pointed the snake's head toward Mitzi's.

There was dead silence in the room as Mitzi stood there, unflinching, while the boa, tongue flicking, reached Mitzi and wrapped itself around her arm.

"I don't believe it," Tracey said out loud.

"Neither do I," echoed Bobbie.

"Hey, Mitzi, better watch your neck. Bruno may not be too little for you," said Jason.

The class laughed, but it was a different kind of laughter this time. It wasn't against Mitzi; it was for her.

"What does the snake feel like, Mitzi?" Margie asked.

"Cool. Dry." Mitzi answered. "Rather nice."

"He isn't slimy?" asked another girl named Kiki.

"No. Not at all."

"Is he wrapped very tight?" someone else wanted to know.

"No. Not too tight."

The class asked a few more questions. Then Margie said, "I think you're awfully brave."

"Unlike some other people we know who were too scared to hold him," said Janet, looking at the Monkey Trio.

The rest of the class looked at them, too, and laughed.

Except Mitzi. She stood straight and tall, patting Bruno, still wound around her arm.

Mrs. Livetti finished the drawing, took the snake from Mitzi, and slipped him back in his case.

The class copied the drawing while Mrs. Livetti explained it.

"Mitzi, that was terrific," Janet whispered. "You really showed everyone up. You seem so . . . uh . . . different today. Almost like a new person."

"Or perhaps like an old one," Mitzi murmured. "A very old one."

11

All right. Squad One, the horse. Squad Two, the ropes. Squad Three, the parallel bars. Squad Four . . ." Mrs. Vetch glared at Mitzi. ". . . the trampoline."

Mitzi stared right back. Once I faced the Roman army, she told herself. I am not going to let a mere gym teacher upset me now. But then she turned toward the trampoline and her stomach fluttered. The snake had been scary enough. When he'd slid onto her arm, Mitzi'd had to remind herself that Boadicea must have encountered fiercer animals than a baby boa constrictor. But the trampoline. . . . That piece of apparatus had always bugged Mitzi nearly as much as the ropes. Bouncing on it was sort of fun, but you could fall off the edge or get tangled in the springs. Also, Mrs. Vetch always tried to make everyone do fancy stuff like drops, twists, and even somersaults, all of which terrified Mitzi.

Maybe I should tell Mrs. Vetch that I hurt my

knees and I can't. . . . No! Mitzi cut herself off. No! None of that. I who conquered the city of Londinium am not afraid to jump up and down on a trampoline.

She headed toward it.

"At least we don't have to climb the ropes today," Janet, walking next to her, murmured comfortingly.

"Never mind. The trampoline will do," Mitzi said.

"Do? Do what?"

Mitzi didn't answer. She watched silently as Ricky Horton, who was as good on the trampoline as he was on the ropes, got on it first. Her eyes burned fiercely as she watched him bounce high and execute a perfect triple cat twist. The other spotters gasped. Mitzi didn't say a word.

"Excellent," Mrs. Vetch said, while the rest of the squad applauded. Then she turned to Mitzi. "All right, Meyer," she said. "Let's see you tackle the trampoline."

The Monkey Trio, as usual, giggled. Janet, also as usual, told Mitzi she could do it. And Ricky flashed another one of his encouraging smiles.

Mitzi ignored all of them. I carried a spear. I rode a chariot into battle. I slew legions of Romans by my own hand. I refused to be a slave, she thought as she hoisted herself up on the rubbery sheet, stood, and walked to the center in one swift motion. She gave a little shudder and hoped no one saw it. Then, without further hesitation, she began to bounce, just lightly as first, up and down, up and down. Then harder and faster. *Boing, boing!*

"Go, Mitzi, go!" Janet cheered. "Touch your toes."

Mitzi knew that she meant she should stretch out her arms and kick her legs up high to the sides so that her toes tapped her fingers. It was something she'd never done before because she'd been too worried about landing on her rump. But now she yelled, "Charge!" and *boing, kick, boing, kick!* She touched her toes twice. She turned her head and saw Janet grinning at her. She wanted to grin back, but it didn't seem queenly.

"Not bad," she heard Mrs. Vetch say. "Now let's see you do swivel-hips."

Swivel-hips! That meant dropping to your seat, giving a half twist in the air so that your hips rotated and doing a second seat drop. Mitzi had seen other people do it, but she'd never done it herself.

"You can do it," Janet said.

"Yes, Mitzi. Give your hips a swivel," said Tracey.

Bobbie and Diane laughed.

"All right," said Mitzi. And suddenly she went bounce, drop, swivel, drop and, before anyone had time to take a second breath, she did a full twist and another seat drop before she landed neatly on her feet.

"Wow!" said Bobbie Bolen.

"Wow, wow," Jason Pollack chimed in.

This time Janet was too stunned to say anything.

Mitzi, bouncing gently, looked at Mrs. Vetch.

"That was . . . satisfactory," the teacher said grudgingly. "You can get off now. It's Dudeen's turn."

Mitzi, smiling slightly, gave a queenly bow. "Certainly," she said and crouching down at the edge, she held on to the bar and flipped herself over, landing neatly on the mat right next to the teacher.

"Mitzi," Janet said when they were changing after class in the locker room. "I — I — you — I mean, the snake. That was one thing. But the trampoline . . . What *is* going on? There's something you haven't told me. . . ."

Tracey, Bobbie, and Diane, whose lockers were nearby, leaned toward them to hear what Mitzi had to say.

"Not really," Mitzi said loudly.

"But you are a different person, Mitzi. I'm not kidding. Yesterday you were scared of things and today — " Janet broke off.

Mitzi shrugged. "I'm now the person I have

always wanted to be because I became the person I once was."

Janet frowned. Then her eyes opened wide. "Oh! Oh, Mitzi! You didn't! I mean, you did. You went to see — "

"Um-humph," Mitzi warned, gesturing with her eyes at the Monkey Trio.

The bell rang. "We'd better get back to class," Mitzi said.

"Right," said Janet.

As they walked out of the locker room, Mitzi whispered. "I will reveal all — at lunch."

"Oh, Mitzi, I was right! I knew Madame Blini'd help you — and she did," Janet said in the cafeteria after Mitzi'd described her session with the psychic. "She really has amazing powers, doesn't she?"

"She is gre — " Mitzi began. But she cut herself off. It wouldn't do for a queen to sound so enthusiastic. "Gifted," she finished haughtily.

"Oh come on, she knew about you and Boadicea. I'd call that amazing."

"It was somewhat . . . impressive."

"Mitzi! You're teasing me."

"We never tease," Mitzi said the way a queen would.

Janet threw her sandwich bag at her. Mitzi didn't deign to throw it back. She was noticing the Monkey Trio staring at her from a nearby table. She looked back boldly until they had to lower their eyes or turn their heads away.

"I wonder how Boadicea, I mean, I, eliminated her, I mean, my enemies."

"She probably bumped them off," Janet said.

"Yes. What an excellent idea. Although a bit barbaric. Maybe she banished them instead."

"Too bad she didn't have magic powers to turn them into real monkeys."

Mitzi snorted. Then she said, "Lower your voice. They're trying to overhear us. That's all we need — the Monkey Trio going to Madame Blini."

"But Mitzi, what would be so awful about that? Maybe deep inside they want to be nice and. . . ."

"Nice? The Monkey Trio? Come on! Janet, don't you dare tell them about her. Don't you dare." Mitzi heard her voice getting all panicky. Abruptly, she drew herself up. "I command you."

"Yes, Your Highness," Janet answered with a giggle.

Mitzi didn't laugh with her. She gave a nod of her head and glanced toward the trio. "Good. They've stopped listening." She fell silent, then she said, "Well, I suppose for the time being my present plan against them is good enough."

"What's your present plan?" Janet asked.

"Showing them up." This time Mitzi allowed

herself to grin. "Them and" — her eyes scanned the room — "that one."

Janet followed Mitzi's gaze and saw Ricky Horton sitting with a bunch of his friends. "You know, I think you might be wrong about Ricky. Yesterday in gym I think maybe he was just trying to be helpful. I think he really likes you."

Mitzi wasn't listening. She'd just had an idea — a wild one for Mitzi, but not for Boadicea. She got up and walked over to Ricky's table. "Hello, Ricky," she said.

"Hey, it's Mitzi the snake charmer," said Paul Moscowitz, one of the boys at the table.

"She doesn't look like a charming snake to me," Sammy Serrone, another of Ricky's friends, joked.

"Oh hi, Mitzi," Ricky said. "Hey, that was a pretty good twist you did in gym today."

"Yes, it was, wasn't it?" Mitzi said. "But I do not wish to discuss physical education with you. I have come to ask if you are still seeking people to join the scuba diving class."

"The scuba diving class?" said Ricky. "Yeah. Sure. Why?"

"I would like to register for it."

"You would?"

"Yes, I would," Mitzi said firmly, as if she were daring him to contradict her.

"Gee, that's great, Mitzi. That means now we'll have enough people for the class."

"That's too many girls," Paul moaned.

"Yeah," Sammy agreed.

"Who is in the class?" asked Mitzi.

"You, me, Janet, Paul, and Sammy here, Bobbie, Diane, and Tracey," Ricky answered.

Mitzi paused a moment. Then, "Perfect," she said.

"It starts a week from Friday at four-thirty. Is that okay?"

Mitzi nodded.

"Great."

As Mitzi walked away she heard Paul hoot, "Hey, Horton likes charming snakes."

"You should know, Moscowitz," Sammy said. "You've got a face like a python yourself."

"What did you say to him?" Janet asked when Mitzi got back to their table.

"Nothing much. Just that I'm joining your scuba diving class."

"Oh, Mitzi. That doesn't sound like a good way of showing him up."

"Why not?"

"Well, when you don't turn up for class, he'll just think. . . ."

"What makes you think I won't turn up for class?" Mitzi cut her off.

"Mitzi," Janet said seriously. "I think it's great you're becoming the person you always wanted to be and that you're so much braver now, but scuba diving. It . . . it. . . . "

"It what?"

"Well, Mitzi. You don't even know how to swim."

"So what? I didn't know how to do swivel-hips either before today."

"It's not the same thing. It — "

Once again Mitzi drew herself up and fixed her eyes on Janet. "My dear Janet," she said. "Surely you don't think the Queen of the Britons fears a little water!" Then, rising majestically, she gathered up her sandwich wrapper and juice carton and dumped them into a neighboring garbage pail.

Janet watched her. Uh-oh, she thought. Uh-oh.

12

Everybody was talking about Mitzi. But instead of jokes and remarks at her expense, it was now: "Oh, that Mitzi Meyer. Did you see how she jumped over the horse in gym yesterday? Wow!" Or "I saw Mitzi Meyer after school yesterday. She was climbing the biggest tree in the park." Or "You know that humongous dog that hangs out at Newcomb's? The one everyone's afraid of? Guess who I saw petting him this morning? Mitzi Meyer." "She's amazing." "She sure is." "What do you think happened to her? She didn't used to be like that." "I don't know, but I'm inviting her to my birthday party next week." "I'm inviting her to the amusement park tomorrow." "She's the most popular kid in our class now. She's even more popular than Ricky Horton."

If Ricky Horton minded, he wasn't saying. In fact he was one of the only kids in the class who didn't talk about Mitzi, although he seemed to wear a slightly puzzled look when he heard the others talk about her. But Ricky's lack of gossip was more than made up for by the Monkey Trio who talked about practically nothing but Mitzi Meyer. They were convinced Mitzi had pulled a fast one on them and everyone else.

"She's got to have some kind of weird secret. Nobody changes that fast," Diane said at the end of the week.

"Maybe it's not really her," said Bobbie.

"What do you mean?"

"Well, I saw this movie once about twins. One was really shy and nice. The other was a holy terror. Maybe Mitzi isn't really Mitzi, but her twin."

Diane clucked her tongue. "Yeah? And where's she been hiding this twin all this time? In the basement?"

"Well, Miss Foster, you come up with a better idea."

"Witchcraft," said Diane.

"Huh?"

"She's been practicing black magic, and, boom, some devil got into her."

"But she doesn't have green skin or red eyes," said Bobbie.

"What's that got to do with it?"

"Didn't you see *The Exorcist?*"

"That dumb movie — "

"Girls, please," Tracey stopped them. "There's only one way to find out why and how Mitzi has changed."

"What's that?" asked Bobbie.

"We ask."

"We ask Mitzi? She won't tell us."

"No, that's true. Mitzi won't. But Janet might."

"Janet? She's Mitzi's best friend. She won't say anything either," said Diane.

"I think she might. Maybe not right now. But soon. Very soon."

"Why? Why should she?"

Tracey gave a knowing smile. "If your best friend went from a scaredy cat to Wonder Woman over-night, how do you think you'd feel?"

"Confused," said Bobbie.

"Weird," said Diane.

"Right. But you also might feel angry — especially if she acted like she didn't need you any-more."

"You think Mitzi's acting like that?"

"Look."

Diane and Bobbie turned their heads just in time to see Mitzi come into the class. She looked tall. Very tall, and very superior.

"Mitzi!"

"Hi, Mitzi!"

"Want some gum, Mitzi?"

"Wanna go to the park after school?"

Mitzi nodded and smiled benevolently at everyone, saying "yes" or "no, thank you" as she glided toward her seat.

Janet trailed behind her. She wasn't smiling at anyone. She was sort of frowning.

"Mitzi, do you want to come over to my house today and see my brother's snake?" Freda asked.

"Oh, I would enjoy that, but today I'm going to help my dear neighbor, Mrs. Pleasant, in her garden," Mitzi replied.

"You are?" said Janet. "You didn't tell me that."

"I must've forgotten."

"I didn't even know you liked gardening."

"I do — especially digging up those nice, long worms."

Some of the kids heard that and laughed, but Janet only frowned again.

"Hey, Mitzi, do you want to go to Wowee Amusement Park tomorrow?" Kiki Montgomery asked. Kiki wasn't pretty, but she was popular because of her bouncy personality. In the past, Mitzi had thought she might like to be Kiki's friend, but Kiki'd never paid any attention to her.

"Tomorrow? I believe I can. My father and I are supposed to climb Bentner Tower this weekend, but I'm sure we can do that on Sunday."

"Great!" said Kiki. "My father will pick you up tomorrow at eleven."

"That's fine. Janet, you can be at my house by then, can't you?"

"What? Huh? Wait a minute, Mitzi. I don't know if I want to go to Wowee tomorrow," Janet protested.

"Oh gee, I'm not sure there's room in the car," Kiki said at the same time.

"It'll be fun," Mitzi said to Janet. "We can go on the Typhoon together. You will come, won't you?" And to Kiki, "Janet's not big. She can sit on my lap."

"Oh. Okay," Kiki said.

"All right," said Janet, with another frown.

"See what I mean?" said Tracey to Diane and Bobbie.

"Uh-huh," they both agreed.

"But how do we get Janet to talk?" asked Diane.

"We could tickle her — that always works on my sister," said Bobbie.

Diane clucked her tongue again. "I didn't mean that kind of how. I meant what's the set-up?"

"Tea," said Tracey.

"Huh?" said Bobbie and Diane together.

"And cookies. On Sunday afternoon."

"Oh."

"I'll invite her myself. Right after school."

Janet was the only one in Mrs. Livetti's class (besides Ricky Horton) who didn't talk about Mitzi.

But she decided it was about time she talked *to* her. Her best friend was, as the Monkey Trio noticed, getting on her nerves. It was nice to see her once timid friend now so brave and bold. But there's such a thing as overdoing it, Janet thought.

So, on Friday, as she and Mitzi were leaving school, she said, "Mitzi, I have something to say to you."

"About what, pray tell?" Mitzi asked.

"It's about that. About the way you're talking these days."

"The way I'm talking? What objection, my dear Janet, could you possibly have to my speech?"

"It's, well . . . it's a little . . . uh . . . fancy, don't you think? For everyday conversation?"

"Not for a queen's everyday conversation."

Grr, Janet wanted to growl. But calmly she said, "And there's also some of the things you've been doing. Like climbing that tree yesterday."

"That was most enjoyable."

"That was most dangerous. Some of those branches weren't too sturdy. They could've broken."

"They didn't."

"But they could have. . . . Oh, Mitzi. You're brave now. Really brave. I know it. The other kids know it. Even better, you know it. But you don't have to take risks to prove it."

"Boadicea has nothing to prove."

Janet sighed. "Mitzi, you're not Boadicea."

Mitzi's eyes darkened. "What do you mean I am not Boadicea? You know what Madame Blini said."

"She meant you were *once* Boadicea. But not now. . . ."

"Untrue! You told me yourself that what you once were you still are."

"Well, yes — and no. You keep some of the traits from your past lives — and you can be some of those things, like brave or strong. But you're not the same person. Look, you're not living in ancient Britain. You don't drive a chariot. You don't lead an army. And Mitzi, you're not a queen."

Mitzi gave her a look that would've shriveled any peasant who dared question her authority back in 62 A.D.

"You are wrong, Janet Jellinco. Once a queen — always a queen," said Mitzi imperiously. "Now, if you will excuse me, I must help dear Mrs. Pleasant. It is my duty." And she strode away.

"*Grrr.*" This time Janet did growl. "*Grrr.*" If she doesn't stop this queen business soon, I'll . . . crown her. She thinks she's so special. Everybody's just as special. Why, if the rest of the kids went to Madame Blini, some of them might turn out to be kings and queens, too. Maybe even emperors.

Janet's thoughts were interrupted by a lazy voice that called, "Oh, Janet!" She turned around.

Tracey Dudeen was walking toward her. "Hi," she said. "Did I interrupt you and Mitzi?"

"No," said Janet warily.

"It seemed as though you were having a little . . . tiff."

"No, it was nothing like that."

"Oh. Well. I want to invite you over on Sunday afternoon at three for tea."

"Tea?"

"That's what I call it — although it's really lemonade and cookies." Tracey smiled.

"Oh. Thank you for the invitation, but I don't think I can come. I think I'm busy," Janet said, still wary.

"Well, if you change your mind, here's my address." She handed Janet a slip of paper. "And I do hope you change your mind. You see, I think it's about time we became friends. We have so much in common."

"We do?"

Tracey smiled again. "See you soon." She walked away.

Janet looked after her and shrugged. What was that all about, she wondered. Then she began walking home slowly. Well, Mitzi, she said to herself, I'm going to give you one more chance. And if you don't start acting like a friend instead of a Royal Highness, I'm going to do something that knocks you off your throne.

99

13

Isn't this the most spectacular view you ever saw?"

"Spectacular," Mitzi agreed. She was standing next to her father at the top of Bentner Tower surveying the landscape spread out below them. She felt dizzy but she didn't tell him that. I'll be all right, she told herself as she had done all week. Queen Boadicea is not afraid of heights. And sure enough, once again she was fine.

A blue jay flew below her, making a noise like a rusty hinge. "I'm higher than you are, bird," she said to it.

"I'm proud of you, Mitzi," her father said. "And you should be proud of yourself. You've conquered your fear of heights."

"Yes," said Mitzi. "I have conquered many things. I have reached the very pinnacle of success."

Mr. Meyer laughed. "You're quite a card, Mitzi Meyer."

Although she hadn't been joking, she was glad

her father appreciated her at last. Unlike some other people she could name — namely Michael and Janet.

Michael had been giving her funny looks all week, asking her if she felt okay and acting worried. She assured him over and over she was fine. She didn't tell him about Madame Blini. She still didn't want anyone else to know about her. She was even sorry she'd told Janet she'd gone to her. On Friday morning, Michael stopped giving her looks and actually insulted her. It was after she'd told him she no longer wished to be called "Spike." "It doesn't befit a queen," she said.

He stared at her for a moment and then said, "Then how about if I call you Snotty. That's more 'befitting.' "

"How dare you insult me," Mitzi said coldly.

Michael gave her the saddest look she'd ever seen. "I don't get it, Mitzi. How come you're acting like this? It's like you're not my sister anymore. You're somebody I don't even know."

Mitzi felt as though he'd slapped her. She wanted to say something to him, but she didn't know what. How did a queen talk to her brother? Mitzi didn't know. So she didn't say anything at all, and eventually he left the room, his shoulders hunched and his head lowered. For the rest of the weekend, he'd avoided her.

Then yesterday, it was Janet who was upset

with her. It was a lovely day, sunny and breezy, perfect for Wowee Amusement Park. Janet showed up on time at Mitzi's house. She seemed grumpy, though, especially when they piled into Kiki's father's car, but Mitzi didn't think it was a serious bad mood. They got to the park easily and were able to get the tickets for all the rides they wanted to go on, which, in Mitzi's case, was just about all the rides — particularly the scary ones like the Whirling Dervish, the Zoom-to-Doom, the Plunger and, most of all, the Typhoon. Mitzi insisted on riding the roller coaster three times. Janet didn't object until Mitzi decided she wanted to go on it once more.

Then Janet flatly refused. "Uh-uh. That's it for me," she said.

"But Janet," Mitzi said. "I thought you loved the Typhoon."

"I do, but not four times in one day."

"I'll go on it again with you, Mitzi," Kiki said.

Mitzi smiled in a queenly fashion at her. "Thank you, Kiki." She turned back to Janet and, in a most unqueenly fashion, said, "Come on, Janet. Don't be a stick-in-the-mud."

Quietly, Janet answered, "No."

Mitzi drew herself up. "Surely, my dear Janet, you have not suddenly become afraid of a little Typhoon." Mitzi joked the way she thought Boadicea might.

"No, I'm not afraid of it," Janet answered curtly.

"I didn't think so. You may not be a queen, but you are certainly not a coward." Mitzi smiled.

Instead of smiling back, Janet snapped, "That's it, Mitzi. That's the last straw." She stomped away, leaving Mitzi standing alone with a bewildered look on her face.

Mitzi didn't see her for the rest of the afternoon until four o'clock when Kiki's father met them in the parking lot. And then Janet wouldn't even talk to her the whole ride home.

Mitzi didn't understand it. Janet and Michael, the two people she thought would appreciate her new personality more than anyone else, seemed to be angry with her. She'd even tried to invite Janet to Bentner Tower this morning. But Mrs. Jellinco answered the phone and said that Janet was busy and couldn't talk. Doesn't Janet understand that I am a queen, Mitzi wondered. She's just a teacher, according to Madame Blini. She can talk and act any old way. But I must speak and act — nobly. Everyone must look up to me. That's what it means to be a queen, doesn't it?

"Ready to climb down?" her father asked.

Mitzi gave herself a little shake. "Oh. Yes," she said. She looked over the side of the tower once more. "What's that?" She pointed to a narrow rocky path cutting through the cliff below. "Is that another way to get down?"

Mr. Meyer looked where she was pointing. "Yes. But it's much more difficult than the one we took up to the tower. It cuts through the rocks. It's quite a scramble."

"Let's take it," said Mitzi.

"You sure?"

"Certainly."

Mr. Meyer laughed. "Mitzi, you're something else. One minute you're scared of everything, the next you're ready to take on the world. All right, then, let's do it."

They bounded down the tower steps together.

The path *was* a scramble — crawling under, over, even between crags, boulders and outcroppings of rock. In one spot was a narrow ledge over a twenty-five-foot-deep gorge. But Mitzi crossed it as though it were the street she lived on. When they finally reached the bottom, her father praised her again and told her he was looking forward to going to Muckamucka Falls with her soon.

Muckamucka Falls was a place Mitzi had always been petrified of. But now she wouldn't be. She nodded and smiled, basking in her father's praise and pleasure.

On the way home she told herself that everything was just about perfect. I can't wait to tell Janet that I climbed Bentner Tower, she thought. And won't Michael be impressed that Dad and I climbed down that steep path instead of the easier one. I hope they're not still jealous. Surely they'll have gotten over that by —

"Mitzi," Mr. Meyer interrupted her thoughts. "Isn't that your friend Janet?" he said.

Mitzi looked out the window. Sure enough, it was Janet, walking purposefully a little way ahead of them on Blossom Street.

Mitzi called out, "Janet! My dear Janet!"

But Janet didn't seem to hear her. She kept walking, and as Mitzi watched, she turned into the driveway of a house and up the front path.

I wonder who she's visiting, Mitzi thought. She doesn't have any friends on Blossom Street.

As they drove past, Mitzi turned her head just in time to see the front door of the house open and a girl come out to greet Janet.

The girl was Tracey Dudeen.

14

Mitzi, want to go on a picnic next Saturday?"
"Mitzi, will you show me how you did that inside-out position on the parallel bars today?"

"Hey, Mitzi, here's a picture of something I bet you'd love to do — *spelunking*. That means crawling around in a dark cave wearing a miner's hat with a little light on it."

Monday morning, and to Mitzi everything was still perfect — except for the fact that Michael was still avoiding her and that Janet hadn't walked to school with her. She turned to Paul Moscowitz. "Spelunking does sound fascinating. But personally, I think I'd prefer climbing the outside of the cave rather than the inside." She shifted her glance to Ricky Horton.

He wasn't looking at her.

Mitzi gave a little frown and turned to some of her other admirers. She was so busy letting them offer compliments, invitations and even small gifts (a pencil, a barrette, another stick of gum) that she didn't see Janet come in. But when Mitzi finally turned her head again, there she was, in the seat next to hers.

"Janet!" Mitzi said.

Janet mumbled hello.

"Is that all you're going to say? Where were you this morning?" Mitzi asked. Then, suddenly aware that the rest of the class was watching her, she drew herself up and said, "I suppose you overslept."

"No, I didn't," Janet said curtly.

"I hope you had no difficulties at home."

"None."

"Oh."

Mitzi was feeling even more puzzled and hurt than she had been the day before. Jason and Sammy arrived and greeted her. She wanted to continue talking to Janet, but she felt it would be rude not to greet them.

"My sister saw you at Bentner Tower yesterday," Jason said. Everyone knew Jason's sister. She was the school crossing guard. "She said you were coming down the old Slide Path with your dad."

"That's right."

"The old Slide Path! That's really tricky," said Sammy admiringly.

"It was — invigorating." She smiled at them

and turned back to Janet. "I called you to come along, but your mother said you were busy."

"I was," said Janet.

Mitzi paused, then said, "I guess you were busy in the afternoon, too."

"Yes."

Mitzi waited for her to explain, but when she didn't, Mitzi said, "I thought I saw you on my return from the tower. You were walking up Blossom Street."

Janet still said nothing, so Mitzi had to go on. "Ridiculous as it seems, I thought I saw you visit Tracey Dudeen." She paused.

"I did visit Tracey," Janet finally said. "I was invited for tea along with Bobbie and Diane."

"Tea? With the Monkey Trio?" Mitzi said, her voice rising. "What'd you eat? Bananas?"

The class looked at her again. She smiled at them and kept smiling as she said in a lower voice, "Janet, my dear. You seem to be keeping strange company these days."

"I sure am," Janet said, staring right at Mitzi.

Kiki overheard and giggled.

Mitzi glared at her.

"Anyway, I think you'll soon find the Monkey Trio — I mean, Tracey, Diane, and Bobbie — aren't the same as they used to be."

"What do you mean?"

108

"You'll see," was all Janet would say. "Here they come now."

Mitzi looked up and her mouth fell open. There in the doorway stood the Monkey Trio, dressed all in white: white dresses, white stockings, white hats, white shoes, even white lace gloves. They each carried a white daffodil and wore identical white-toothed smiles. And they headed straight for Mitzi.

"Oh, Mitzi! Mitzi Meyer! We're so pleased to see you," said Diane.

"Yes, we truly are," agreed Bobbie.

"I'll bet," Mitzi muttered.

They beamed at her.

"We have most humbly come to ask you for your forgiveness. You will forgive us, won't you?" asked Tracey.

"What?" Mitzi asked sharply.

"We must love our enemy, Mitzi," said Diane. "Love is the Golden Rule."

"Do unto others as you would have them do unto you," intoned Tracey.

"Love is all you need."

"Love thy neighbor."

"A stitch in time saves nine."

"What?" Tracey and Diane looked at Bobbie. She shrugged. "I had to write that one hundred times last year." Tracey and Diane both clucked their tongues.

109

Then all three of them smiled again at Mitzi and, on a signal from Tracey, laid their daffodils on her desk.

Mitzi closed her eyes. This must be a dream, she thought. But when she opened her eyes, the flowers — and the Monkey Trio—were still there. What are they up to, she thought. She felt the other kids staring at them. She had to say something. "Thank you for the charming gift," she finally said.

"You're welcome," Tracey said. She, Diane, and Bobbie took their seats. The other kids whispered among themselves, about what Mitzi didn't know.

Confused and wary, Mitzi looked at Janet.

Janet stared right back at her with a big smirk on her face.

At lunchtime Mitzi was itching to talk to Janet. But Janet wasn't at their usual table. She was sitting with Margie and Freda. Mitzi got up to join them, but before she could, the Monkey Trio surrounded her.

"If your enemy offends you, turn the other cheek," said Tracey.

"Love is the reason you were born," said Diane.

"Here, Mitzi. We've brought you your lunch," Bobbie told her, pushing her gently down into her seat with one hand and setting down the tray with the other.

110

Mitzi looked suspiciously at it. "What's in it? Arsenic?" she asked, forgetting who she was.

"No, tuna salad," said Bobbie.

"You do like tuna salad, don't you?" asked Diane.

"It's . . . satisfactory," Mitzi answered.

"We want you to know how sorry we are for the terrible things we used to say to you," said Tracey.

"Even if they were true," added Bobbie.

Tracey and Diane gave her a look, then, smiling, they all sat down.

Mitzi nodded politely at them and ate a forkful of tuna salad. The Monkey Trio watched her and said nothing.

Mitzi took another forkful. The Monkey Trio kept watching. Finally, Mitzi said, "Aren't you going to eat?"

"Oh no," explained Tracey. "We're fasting today. To purify our bodies and our spirits."

They sure need a lot of purifying, Mitzi thought.

"That's what saints do," added Bobbie.

"Saints?" said Mitzi.

"Oh, yes," put in Diane.

Mitzi was beginning to feel nauseous as well as suspicious. She tried to eat a little more of the tuna salad but, even for a queen, it felt weird eating alone while three people dressed in white stared at you.

A few other kids came by to greet Mitzi, but no one else sat down. She looked longingly at Janet, but Janet seemed to be involved in a very animated conversation with Margie and Freda.

Mitzi didn't feel like eating anymore. She pushed her tray away. Bobbie quickly whisked it off the table and went to return it.

"It is such a pleasure to serve you," said Tracey.

"Such a pleasure," repeated Diane.

Mitzi tried to give them a regally gracious smile, but she had the distinct feeling it came out crooked.

At two-fifty-five, Mitzi had it all planned. As soon as the bell rang, she was going to rush over to Janet's desk and ask what was going on. But then Mrs. Livetti asked her if she'd stay a few minutes extra to wash the blackboard, and she couldn't very well refuse. It wasn't until three-ten that she finally left the classroom. Janet hadn't waited for her. But the Monkey Trio had.

"We're going to walk you home," Bobbie told her.

Mitzi didn't say anything. She was getting rather fed up with her entourage.

Outside the school she saw Janet, Margie, and Freda. This time the three of them were talking to Kiki Montgomery. Mitzi took a few steps toward them and realized the Monkey Trio was following her. "Wait here," she commanded, pointing at the ground.

They smiled and obeyed.

Mitzi had to force herself not to run over to Janet, but she walked as quickly as she could while still maintaining her dignity. "Janet," she said. "I want to talk with you."

Janet ignored her.

"Janet!" she repeated.

Finally Janet turned. "I am sorry, my dear Mitzi. I am otherwise engaged."

"Oh. Well, how about later?"

"I doubt it," said Janet. She turned back to the other girls.

Mitzi stood there for a moment, feeling awful. Then she headed toward her house. It wasn't until she got there that she realized the Monkey Trio had followed her the whole way.

Suddenly Mitzi whirled to them. "All right. That's enough. The joke's over."

"Why, Mitzi, what do you mean?" asked Diane.

"I know you hate me, but I didn't think you'd carry it this far."

"We don't hate you, Mitzi," said Tracey.

"We used to, but we don't anymore," Bobbie put in.

"Following me around, giving me flowers, getting me my lunch. I mean, I know I once was a queen, but you don't and. . . ."

"Yes we do," the Monkey Trio said. "You were Queen Boadicea."

"How do you know that?" Mitzi gawped. "Who told you?"

"Janet," said Diane.

"Janet! She wouldn't. . . ." Mitzi stopped. She remembered Janet's recent actions. She would, she thought. That traitor!

"Yes," said Tracey. "She was angry at you. But in the end she helped us all. She helped us become who we want to be by discovering who we once were."

Mitzi had a sinking feeling in her stomach. She didn't really want to ask the next question, but she had to. "And just how did Janet do that?"

"She told us about Madame Blini," Tracey replied.

"We all went to her. Oh, she was so amazing," said Diane. "She told us the truth about ourselves."

Mitzi didn't ask them what the truth was, but Bobbie told her anyway.

"She took one look at us and said we were saints. We thought she'd tell us we were queens like you, or, better still, empresses. But she said we were much holier than that and not to forget it. She was very firm about it."

Mitzi coughed. "That's ridiculous! You, saints? You. . . ." She broke off. It did seem ridiculous, but if Madame Blini told them that, it was also true. Madame Blini wouldn't lie, would she? Madame Blini always told the truth. Mitzi stood there, feeling confused.

Then Diane said, "We are so happy Madame Blini helped us that we are going to help others be happy too."

Mitzi, still confused, just stared at her.

"Yes. We are going to give everyone the opportunity to transform into great beings," said Tracey.

"Wh-what?" Mitzi asked.

"We're gonna tell everybody about Madame Blini," said Bobbie.

"Oh no" was all Mitzi could say. "Oh no."

15

"Hey, Mitzi, think our squad's going on the trampoline again today?"

"Say, Mitzi, did you see that new movie at the Strand?"

"Hey, Mitzi, don't forget the scuba diving class starts this Friday."

Mitzi smiled and nodded at everyone, but she noticed there were fewer people greeting her and that some people weren't greeting her at all.

In another moment she realized why. There were three new students in Mrs. Livetti's class: a movie star, a cowgirl, and a wild woman.

"Hello, dahling Mitzi," said the movie star, who used to be homely Kiki Montgomery. "So mahvelous to see you. I won't forget you when I go to Hollywood." She adjusted her rhinestone sunglasses with one hand and waved her long cigarette holder with the other.

"Well, howdy, Mitzi," said the cowgirl (a.k.a. Margie Fridley) in her fringed vest and ten-gallon hat. "I've jest been as eager as a pony in a new pasture to see you."

"Unh," said the wild woman. It took Mitzi several seconds to realize that under the frizzy hair and fake leopard skin dress was Freda Bauer.

"What's with them?" asked Jason loudly.

"I don't know," answered Sammy.

Mitzi knew, and she was staring at them all in dismay. She thought Freda, Kiki, and Margie looked even more ridiculous than the Monkey Trio did in their white outfits and that they were acting more ridiculously, too. Perhaps as queen I ought to have a chat with them, Mitzi thought, then frowned. She suddenly felt that same confused feeling she'd had the day before about Madame Blini and the Truth. She went silently to her desk.

Then the Monkey Trio came in. They took one look at Margie, Kiki, and Freda and said, "Madame Blini?"

"Madame Blini," nodded Margie.

"Isn't she amazing?"

"Amazin'. You'll jest never guess what she told me."

"That you used to live in the Wild West," said Bobbie.

"Why, that's right. I rode the range in Texas. I went on long cattle drives and chased rustlers and had wonderful adventures."

"I was a movie star in the 1930's. I made wonderful movies," said Kiki.

"What did *she* do?" asked Diane, pointing to Freda.

"She was a cave woman in the Ice Age. She had wonderful . . . wonderful. . . . What did you have that was wonderful, Freda?"

"Unh," Freda grunted.

"What's that mean?"

"Dirt," Freda said plainly, then grunted again.

"Amazing," said Diane.

Mitzi sighed and turned her head to see Janet looking at her with a curious expression.

Mitzi quickly turned her head back. Traitor, she thought again. I now brand you an Enemy of the Queen. But the idea didn't make her feel any better. Somehow I don't think this is going to be one of my favorite days, she said to herself.

She was right.

But the next day was worse. Only two kids greeted Mitzi when she came in, and besides one cowgirl, one movie star, one cave woman, three saints, and a queen, Mrs. Livetti's class now contained two knights, one doctor, and the Egyptian architect who designed the pyramids. Madame Blini was on everyone's lips. And Mitzi was more confused and upset than ever.

She wasn't the only one who was confused and

upset. Mrs. Livetti was beginning to be quite concerned over what was going on in her class. So far no one had told her about Madame Blini, but Mitzi feared it was only a matter of time before someone did, and then what would happen?

The parents were unnerved by their children's behavior as well. Mitzi knew that because when she got home after school on Wednesday, Kiki's and Freda's mothers were there. Mitzi heard them talking to her mother in the living room. She didn't go into the room, but she stayed near the doorway to listen.

"Michelle, all Freda does is grunt," Mrs. Bauer was saying. "I've told her so many times that girls must be neat and clean. And now she's wearing this old rag I gave her for Halloween all the time, and she hasn't taken a bath for three days. She's acting like a boy."

"You think that's a problem? Kiki doesn't want to come out of the bath," Mrs. Montgomery griped. "She's used up gallons of bubble bath and bath oil and bars of scented soap. And last night I found her sleeping in my best negligee. It's black satin. I ask you, black satin on an eleven year old!"

"Has Mitzi been acting weird too?" Mrs. Bauer asked.

Mitzi edged a little closer to the doorway.

"Well, she hasn't been dressing strangely. And her bathing habits haven't changed. But her personality has. She used to be afraid of a lot of things. Lately she's been positively fearless. To be honest, it worries me a little. I don't want her to become reckless as well."

"What do you think made her change?" Mrs. Montgomery asked.

"I don't know. She did have some trouble in gym — it was right after that that it happened."

"Well, Freda hasn't had any trouble in gym or anyplace else."

"Neither has Kiki. At least not that I know of. But I suppose I'd better call Mrs. Livetti — just in case."

"That's a good idea," agreed Mrs. Bauer. "We'll both call her."

They got up to leave. Mitzi scooted away from the door and up to her room, where she sat, her stomach sinking further.

By Thursday, it was clear to Mitzi that most of the class had gone to Madame Blini. Only Ricky Horton and a few other kids were acting (and dressing) normally. The principal, Dr. Fletcher, came into their room and demanded to know just what was going on.

No one said a word.

"Mrs. Livetti and I have been getting phone call after phone call from your parents asking what on earth we're teaching you here in school. I tell them we've been teaching you nothing. . . . I mean, this isn't a circus, students. It isn't a carnival. What the devil is going on here?"

"Unh," answered Freda.

"What was that, young lady?"

"She said we've become who we were by becoming who we are," said Sammy.

"No, dummy. I mean, dahling," said Kiki. "We've become who we want to be by becoming who we once were."

"That's not it either," said Jason. "We. . . ."

"Quiet! What are you all talking about?" Dr. Fletcher demanded.

Everybody fell silent again.

The principal's eyes scanned the room and lit on Ricky Horton. He knew Ricky well — he and Ricky's dad were good friends. He thought Ricky was a sensible boy. "Ricky," he asked, "do you know what's going on here?"

"Not really, Dr. Fletcher," Ricky answered uncomfortably.

The principal frowned and looked at the class again. "Well, whatever's going on has got to stop. I'm going to get to the root of this if I have to meet with all of your parents."

Mitzi frowned, too. She wanted to know what was going on as well. There was one person who could tell her. Madame Blini. Mitzi decided it was time to pay her another visit — and soon.

16

Mitzi was changing into her bathing suit at the Y. It was Friday and she'd planned to go see Madame Blini that afternoon, but then she remembered the scuba diving class. I'll see her first thing tomorrow. She'll explain everything. I just know she will, Mitzi thought. In the meantime, I must not worry. I am brave and strong. I am Mitzi Meyer, Fearless Warrior Queen, she told herself once again. But this time a little voice in her head whispered back, Are you?

Mitzi didn't like that voice. She didn't like it at all. Yes, I am, she answered it, and she marched out of the locker room toward the pool. As she neared it, she heard somebody talking. Mitzi recognized the voice. It belonged to Ricky Horton.

"I can't understand what's happening to everybody," he was saying. "It's like they've all gone crazy — even Sammy and Paul. Sammy keeps saying he's Sir Galaramus, Knight of the Royal Garter, and Paul thinks he's some explorer who discovered the world was round before Columbus did. They said some lady named Madame Blini told them that stuff and that I should go to her, too, and then I'd understand."

"I'm afraid it's all my fault," another voice said. Mitzi knew that one too, very well indeed. It was Janet's.

"Your fault? What do you mean?"

"I'm the one who told them about Madame Blini. Well, I didn't actually tell them. I told the Monkey . . . I mean, I told Diane, Bobbie, and Tracey, and they told them."

"Why did you do that?" Ricky asked. "Do you believe in this Madame Blini, too?"

"Well, yes, I do. Or at least I did. But the real reason I told them has to do with Mitzi."

"Mitzi?"

"Yes. You see she went to Madame Blini, and now she thinks she's a fearless warrior queen."

"She does? She believes that stuff too?"

Mitzi felt her temper flare. *I am a fearless warrior queen, you rat finks. I am, I am, I. . . .*

"Hail to you, Mitzi," two voices behind her chorused.

She jumped and spun around. Diane and Bobbie were standing there — in white bathing suits.

"Oh, did we startle you?" asked Diane. "We are sorry."

Mitzi didn't respond to that. Instead, she said, "Where's Tracey?"

"We don't know," said Bobbie.

"She was supposed to meet us out front, but she didn't," Diane said.

They looked disconcerted. Mitzi thought it was strange, too. The Monkey Trio was always inseparable. "She will probably appear later," she said, wanting, in some odd way, to comfort them.

"Yes, she probably will," said Bobbie.

"You are so wise, Mitzi."

Sammy and Paul arrived then as well, and they all walked into the pool room.

Mitzi didn't look at Janet and Ricky when she entered, and she sat down as far away from them as she could.

In another moment, a trim young man who was sitting at the far end of the pool got up and joined them. "Hi," he said. "This is Scuba Diving for Beginners. I'm Ted Fielding, your instructor. Is everyone here? No, I see someone's missing."

"Tracey will be here later," Diane said.

The instructor looked at his sheet. "That's Tracey Dudeen?"

"Yes," said Bobbie.

"Well, we'll wait a few more minutes for her since it's the first class. But in the future we'll start right on time."

They waited, but Tracey didn't appear.

Finally, Mr. Fielding decided to start the class without her. "I hope she does show up," he said. "Or that will give us only seven students." Then he began to talk about scuba diving, what it was, how it began, and what you had to know to do it. Mitzi tried to listen carefully, but she kept thinking about all sorts of other things instead — especially Madame Blini.

". . . swim three hundred yards without fins and stay afloat for fifteen minutes. I'll test you on those things next week," Mr. Fielding finished up. "But first I thought it might be fun for you to see what full scuba gear looks like. How about a volunteer?"

Ricky raised his hand.

Mitzi felt her anger flare up again. "I shall do it," she said, getting to her feet.

The instructor smiled at her. "All right," he said. "Now, we start with the face mask. . . ." He explained what the mask was for and how it was worn. Then he went on to the flippers, the weight belt, the mouthpiece, the harness, the tanks, putting all of the stuff on Mitzi as he talked.

She stood there, feeling heavy and uncomfortable, but uncomplaining. I am a queen, she kept repeating to herself over and over.

"Now that's it. That's the — " Mr. Fielding said.

But he was interrupted by the appearance of Tracey Dudeen.

She was out of breath and her bathing suit straps

were crooked. It crossed Mitzi's mind that her suit was red and not white, but she didn't think much of it until Tracey opened her mouth.

"I'm sorry I'm late," she apologized. "But my parents wanted to talk with me about something very important."

"That's all right, uh, Tracey," Mr. Fielding said. "We — "

But Tracey went on talking. "Something everyone here should know about, especially Mitzi Meyer — wherever she is." She looked confusedly about.

"Mitzi's right there," said Bobbie, pointing at her.

I am a queen, Mitzi said to herself.

Tracey smiled her slow smile. "Oh yes, I should've recognized those feet anywhere."

Mitzi's stomach fluttered. I am a queen, she told it.

"Tracey, how could you?" said Diane, shocked. "Remember who we are."

"Yes, we're saints," said Bobbie.

"Oh no, we're not. We're not saints. We never were. Sammy wasn't a knight. Paul wasn't an explorer. And Mitzi Meyer was certainly no queen."

"What are you talking about?" asked Sammy.

"Yeah," echoed Paul. "I was too an explorer. Madame Blini said so."

"My parents — and some of the other parents,

126

too — did some investigating, and they found out something interesting."

"What?" asked Diane

"They found out Madame Blini is a" — she paused for effect — "charlatan."

"A charlatan? I thought she was a psychic," said Bobbie.

Tracey clucked her tongue. "A charlatan is a fraud, a phony, a big fat fake."

"No!" exclaimed Sammy.

"That couldn't be true," Diane said.

Mitzi let out a gasp, but nobody heard it.

"Oh yes it is. Madame Blini's real name is Rose Rumpowitz. She's a former actress, and she's already been thrown out of six towns. If she doesn't leave this one by tomorrow night, she'll be arrested."

"No!" Sammy said again.

"No, no," Mitzi repeated. It couldn't be. Madame Blini a phony? That meant Mitzi wasn't Queen Boadicea at all. But she had to be. Madame Blini told her she was, and she couldn't have known about Mitzi and the queen if she wasn't a real psychic. Mitzi's head was spinning. She let out a sob. Then she stopped herself. "No," she said out loud. "No, I don't believe it. Madame Blini isn't a fake. She isn't! And I *am* brave and strong. I *am* a queen." Without another word, she jumped into the pool and sank right down to the bottom.

17

There was a robin singing outside Mitzi's window. "Chirrup-cheerily, chirrup-cheerily," it went.

"Shut up, you stupid bird," Mitzi told it. "Don't you know the world stinks?"

After Mr. Fielding had pulled her, gasping and choking, out of the pool and driven her home in his own car, she ran up to her room, pulled the covers over her head, and cried for an hour. Then she just lay there, her spirits as soggy as the rest of her had been a while ago. Finally she'd fallen asleep — and stayed asleep through the rest of the day and the night.

Now it was dawn, a time Mitzi often liked. But not today. Today was the start of the rest of the long, miserable life of Mitzi the Mouse. It was all a lie, all of it, she thought. I was never a queen. I was never brave. I'll never be able to scuba dive or go spelunking or rock climbing or any of those things after all. Ricky and the Monkey Trio and

all the other kids will make fun of me again for-
ever. And now even Janet and Michael will, too.

She felt the tears welling up and reached for a
wad of tissues. I guess I don't really blame them.
I acted pretty dumb. I guess I was pretty snotty,
too. She began to cry again until she fell asleep
once more.

Two hours later, Michael came into her room.
He was carrying a tray. This time there wasn't a
peanut butter and bacon sandwich on it, but a
stack of pancakes.

Mitzi was awake, but she was curled up in a
ball with her back to him.

"Mitzi?" he said.

She didn't answer.

"Mom and Dad have gone for a walk. I brought
you some breakfast."

She said nothing.

"Pear and ginger pancakes. I made them myself. They're not as good as yours, but they're not
bad either."

Mitzi stirred slightly, but she still didn't say a
word.

"I heard what happened with this Madame Blini.
I just want you to know I'm sorry you feel
bad. . . ."

Suddenly, Mitzi sat up. "I hate Madame Blini!
I hate her! She lied to me! She lied to everybody!"

Michael stood there quietly.

"Do you know what she told me? She told me I was a fearless warrior queen. Ha! Isn't that a laugh? Me, Mitzi the Mouse, who's afraid of her own shadow."

Michael was silent for another moment, then he said, "But Mitzi, you have been fearless. You climbed the ropes and jumped on the trampoline and rode the Typhoon four times, didn't you? At least you said you did."

Mitzi remembered how she'd bragged at dinner about those things. Grimacing, she nodded.

"And you climbed Bentner Tower with Dad and even took the Slide Path down. He talked about it for days."

Mitzi nodded again.

"Well, how come you were able to do those things if you're such a mouse?"

"I don't know," Mitzi said in a low voice.

They were both silent for a while. Suddenly, Mitzi leaped out of bed and began throwing on her clothes. "I've got to go," she said.

"Where?" Michael asked.

Mitzi didn't answer. She started for the door, then turned back. "I think I need some nourishment first," she said and wolfed down the pancakes. When she finished, she said, "Those were delicious. Thanks — Mike."

"You're welcome — Spike."

They smiled at each other shyly, but warmly.

130

"Will you tell Mom and Dad I've gone out, but I'll be back later?"

"Sure, but where are you going?'"

This time Mitzi told him. "To Madame Blini," she said.

"Madame Blini? You just said — "

"I know. And I am mad at her. But I've got to find out some things. Don't tell Mom and Dad that I'm going to see her. They'll be angry."

"But Mitzi, I thought I heard them say that she's leaving town today."

"That's why I've got to hurry and catch her."

"Good luck," Michael called after her as she ran out of her room.

"Thanks," she called back and raced down the stairs and out the door.

Mitzi didn't feel at all frightened as she arrived at Madame Blini's place. She was too angry and too full of questions to be frightened. She knocked with the lion knocker three times and waited. No one answered. She tried again. And again.

"Rats!" she said, feeling her anger deflate. "She is gone. Now I'll never find out." She sat down miserably on the doorstep.

But after a few minutes she had a thought. She got up swiftly and went around the corner into the pawnshop.

The skinny owner was there behind the counter.

He peered over his glasses at her. "Oh, it's you. Finally come to redeem that necklace, have you?"

"No, I haven't come to redeem my necklace. I don't care about it much. I've come to ask you if you've seen Madame Blini. You said you knew her."

The man's eyes shifted behind his glasses. "Madame Blini's gone," he said curtly.

"You mean she's left town already?"

"She's gone," the man repeated stubbornly.

Mitzi had a feeling he wasn't telling her the whole truth. "Where did she go? I want to talk with her. I've *got* to talk with her."

The pawnbroker shook his head.

"Herb, have you seen my slippers?" a husky voice said as a big woman in a purple dress lumbered in from the back room. "I've got to pack them."

"Madame Blini!" Mitzi shouted.

The woman turned and looked at Mitzi. "Oh, brother. Another one. Okay, kid, I'll give you back your five bucks. Herb, gimme a bill. I'll pay you back later."

She eased around the counter toward Mitzi, the bill in her hand, and slapped it into Mitzi's.

"There, we're all even. Now go home, kid."

Mitzi, who'd lost her voice for a moment, blurted out, "No!"

"No? Whaddya mean no? I gave ya the money. What else do ya want?"

"I don't want the money. I want answers."

"Answers? Answers to what?"

"How did you know about me and Boadicea? Why did you tell me I was a queen? How come after you told me I did get brave even though what you told me was a lie?"

Madame Blini scrutinized Mitzi for a moment. Then she said, "Come with me, kid. We'll have a little talk." She walked toward the back room, and Mitzi followed.

The small room had a bed, a bureau, a chair, and not much else. "Herb's," she said. "He's my brother. I've been sleeping here since things got . . . hot." She sat on the bed and motioned Mitzi to the chair. She was silent for a few seconds. "Okay. Let me tell you about a woman named Rose Rumpowitz. She wanted to be an actress, see, in the worst way. But she just wasn't cut out for it. Oh, she got a few bit parts here and there. But when she hit forty-five, she knew she and the big time were never destined to meet. Now when Rose was a kid growing up in Queens, New York, she was good at telling people's fortunes at parties and stuff. She told 'em nice things and made 'em happy because that's one thing Rose always liked to do — make people happy. So she thought why not take that up again and this time make some money off it? Except fortune-telling has no class, if you know what I mean."

Mitzi didn't, but she just let Madame Blini continue.

"So Rose was reading this book *Is There Life After Life After Life?* and she got this idea about telling people she could see into their past lives — what they used to be and what they could become. Or, once in a while, what they should become, like telling a miser he was once the most generous man in the world."

"Or telling three nasty girls they once were saints," Mitzi said.

Madame Blini grinned. "Friends of yours?"

"I wouldn't call them that."

Madame Blini went on, "Rose had always had sharp eyes and ears, and she could figure out people just like that." She snapped her fingers. "So Rose Rumpowitz became Madame Blini, her greatest and longest-running role. She's toured this state and other states, met lots of interesting folks and made a little money and a lot of people happy. She made you happy, right?"

"For a while. But I'm not happy now. And you haven't answered my questions," said Mitzi.

"Okay." Madame Blini sighed. "I saw you in the museum sitting in front of that painting of Boadicea, saying you wished you were brave like her.

I left you a flier. When you came to see me, I told you you were her."

With great disappointment, Mitzi said, "That's it?"

"That's it."

"It really was a lie."

"Yes — and no."

"What do you mean?"

"I mean I can't really see into people's past lives, and I don't know if you were ever Queen Boadicea, but I do know there was a brave person in you just waiting to come out. You see, you really can be the person you want to be if you believe in yourself. You believed you were brave and so you were."

Mitzi thought about what Madame Blini had just said for a minute. Then she said, "Okay, I stopped being afraid of heights and stuff. But then how come I couldn't do other things like scuba dive. I nearly drowned."

Madame Blini stared at her. "Can you swim?"

"No."

"Oy. There are some things even brave people have to learn how to do before they can do other things." She shook her head again. "I didn't think anybody'd do anything dumb, I mean, dangerous because of my 'visions.' I am sorry. I apologize."

Mitzi was silent a while. "Well, I guess I accept your apology," she finally said.

135

Madame Blini smiled. "Spoken like a true queen," she said.

Then Mitzi asked, "Do you think I can be brave again? Even though I'm not Boadicea."

Madame Blini looked at her with a gentle smile. "Kid," she said, "whaddya think?"

18

"W ell," Mitzi said, wistfully staring at the painting of Boadicea in the Chillington Museum. "It was fun while it lasted."

"Fun for you, maybe, but not for me," said Janet, standing next to her. "You were the snottiest queen I've ever met."

"And you've met a lot of them," Mitzi teased.

They both laughed.

"Anyway, it's my fault for telling you about Madame Blini and about past lives," Janet said.

"Yeah, but you didn't know I was going to get so carried away."

They were quiet a minute. Then Mitzi asked, "Do you *still* believe in that reincarnation stuff?"

"I'm not sure," said Janet. "But it doesn't matter. I'm more concerned with the future than the past. The future of our planet. Dr. Slavin says the future's in the stars. Space travel to other planets. But we don't want to make the same mistakes there. That's where the aliens can help us. . . ."

"Aliens? What aliens?"

"Why, the ones Dr. Slavin talks about in *What's a Nice Rangadanga Like You Doing in a Place Like This?* He's met the Rangadanga several times and other aliens, too. He says we can meet them also if we. . . ."

"Janet," Mitzi said calmly. "I don't want to hear about it."

"But it's very interesting. You see, we can prepare ourselves by — "

"Janet, shut up."

Janet did.

After a moment, she said, "Well, it's time for your swimming class anyway."

"Oh no," Mitzi groaned.

"Come on, Mitzi. You promised. It's family swim time now so you can go back and forth across the shallow end of the pool until you get the hang of it. And don't worry about how long it'll take you to learn either. Ricky and I are very patient."

"Ricky? Ricky Horton? That creep! I don't want to have anything to do with him. I'll never forgive him for telling me how brave I was all the time. How could you tell him he could teach me to swim?"

"Mitzi, did it ever occur to you that maybe he really did think you were brave — even before you thought you were Boadicea?"

"That's ridiculous. Everybody in the whole class knows I wasn't."

Janet paused a moment, then said, "It depends on what you think is brave. You were afraid of heights and stuff like that, but you weren't afraid of raising your hand and asking or answering lots of questions in class."

"Huh? So what?"

"So, Ricky hates being called on in class. He's nervous about saying things in case he gets them wrong. He thinks you're tremendously brave because you're not worried about that at all. He also admires you for being able to talk to people. He says that's not so easy for him to do."

"You're kidding?" Mitzi said.

"Nope."

Mitzi paused, then asked, "How do you know?"

"He told me so himself — right before scuba diving class!"

Mitzi winced at the memory. "Well, he probably doesn't think I'm brave now. He probably thinks I'm a big jerk, jumping into the deep end of the pool with I don't know how many pounds of stuff on when I can't even swim."

"No, he doesn't think you were a big jerk," Janet said. "A little jerk, maybe, but not a big one."

Mitzi punched her arm.

"Owww. I was only kidding. Come on, let's go. We've got to get to the pool before family swim time is over."

"When's that?"

"In a couple of hours."

"Oh, I just remembered," Mitzi said quickly. "I've got to do my homework, and Michael wants me to. . . ."

"Mitzi, you can do your homework later."

"But Michael. . . ."

"Mitzi!"

"Oh, all right," Mitzi gave in. "I just hope the Monkey Trio isn't there."

"Don't worry," said Janet. "With your luck they probably will be."

"Thanks a lot," Mitzi said, but she smiled.

Then she and Janet walked out of the portrait gallery. But when they got to the door, Mitzi said, "You go on. I'll catch up in two minutes."

"Mitzi," Janet warned.

"I promise. Two minutes."

"Okay," said Janet, and she went on ahead.

Mitzi turned back into the gallery and walked over to Boadicea. She gazed at the painting for a full sixty seconds. Then she said, "Just because Madame Blini wasn't a real psychic doesn't mean it still can't be true, does it? I could've been you in my past life after all, couldn't I?"

And drawing herself up, Mitzi walked slowly and regally out of the museum.